# SHUT UP
# AND KISS ME

# What Reviewers Say About Julie Cannon's Work

**Wishing on a Dream**

"[The main characters] are well-rounded, flawed and with backstories that fascinated me. Their relationship grows slowly and with bumps along the way but it is never boring. At times it is sweet, tender and emotional, at other times downright hot. I love how Julie Cannon chose to tell it from each point of view in the first person. It gave greater insight into the characters and drew me into the story more. A really enjoyable read."—*Kitty Kat's Book Review Blog*

"This book pulls you in from the moment you pick it up. Keirsten and Tobin are very different, but from the moment they get together, the heat and sexual tension are there. Together they must work through their fears in order to have a magical relationship."—*RT Book Reviews*

**Smoke and Fire**

"Cannon skillfully draws out the honest emotion and growing chemistry between her heroines, a slow burn that feels like constant foreplay leading to a spectacular climax. Though Brady is almost too good to be true, she's the perfect match for Nicole. Every scene they share leaps off the page, making this a sweet, hot, memorable read."—*Curve*

"This book is more than a romance. It is uplifting in a very down-to-earth way and inspires hope through hard-won battles where neither woman is prepared to give up."—*Rainbow Book Reviews*

**I Remember**

"Great plot, unusual twist and wonderful women. …[*I Remember*] is an inspired romance with extremely hot sex scenes and delightful passion."—*Lesbian Reading Room*

**Breaker's Passion**

"…an exceptionally hot romance in an exceptionally romantic setting. …Cannon has become known for her well-drawn characters and well-written love scenes."—*Just About Write*

"Cannon writes about Hawaii beautifully, her descriptions of the landscape will make the reader want to jump on the first plane to Maui."—*Lambda Literary Review*

"Julie Cannon brilliantly alternates between characters, giving the reader just enough backstory to entice, but not enough to overwhelm. Cannon intertwines the luscious landscape of Maui and it's tropical destinations into the story, sending the reader on a sensuous vacation right alongside the characters."—*Cherry Grrl*

**Power Play**

"Cannon gives her readers a high stakes game full of passion, humor, and incredible sex."—*Just About Write*

**Just Business**

"Julie Cannon's novels just keep getting better and better! This is a delightful tale that completely engages the reader. It's a must read romance!"—*Just About Write*

**Heartland**

"There's nothing coy about the passion of these unalike dykes—it ignites at first encounter and never abates. ...Cannon's well-constructed novel conveys more complexity of character and less overwrought melodrama than most stories in the crowded genre of lesbian-love-against-all-odds—a definite plus."—Richard Labonte, *Book Marks*

"Julie Cannon has created a wonderful romance. Rachel and Shivley are believable, likeable, bright, and funny. The scenery of the ranch is beautifully described, down to the smells, work, and dust. This is an extremely engaging book, full of humor, drama, and some very hot, hot sex!"—*Just About Write*

**Unchartered Passage**

"Cannon has given her readers a novel rich in plot and rich in character development. Her vivid scenes touch our imaginations as her hot sex scenes touch us in many other areas. *Uncharted Passage* is a great read."—*Just About Write*

**Heart 2 Heart**

"*Heart 2 Heart* has many hot, intense sex scenes; Lane and Kyle sizzle across the pages. It also explores the world of a homicide detective and other very real issues. Cannon has given her readers a read that's fun as well as meaty."—*Just About Write*

**Descent**

"If you are into bike racing, you'll love this book. If you don't know anything about bike racing, you'll learn about this interesting sport. You'll finish the book with a new respect for the sport and the women who participate in it."—Lambda Literary Review

"Julie Cannon once again takes her readers somewhere many have not been before. This time, it's to the rough and tumble world of mountain bike racing."—*Just About Write*

Visit us at www.boldstrokesbooks.com

# By the Author

# SHUT UP AND KISS ME

*by*

Julie Cannon

2019

**Credits**
Editor: Shelley Thrasher
Production Design: Susan Ramundo
Cover Design By Sheri (hindsightgraphics@gmail.com)

# Dedication

For my Family

# CHAPTER ONE

*Day Zero*
*Phoenix to Sydney, Australia*

"You're going to need these."

I accepted the handful of Valium my BFF Charlotte dropped into my hand just after she stopped at curbside check-in at Sky Harbor Airport. I was two hours from boarding a flight to the other side of the world to spend the next three weeks with my sister and our parents cruising the high seas. Why? Because I'm a good daughter and it's that time of the year again. Time for me to show my respect, pay my dues, and not have to deal with my mother's nonstop guilt trip for the rest of my life if I didn't.

"So, what's the problem?" my neighbor Beth had asked innocently last week. "Sounds like the perfect getaway."

I didn't bore her with the details, but the problems are plenty. First, I hate my sister. She's manipulative, obnoxious, pretentious, and a S-N-O-B. She's shallow, has her therapist and yoga instructor on speed dial, and has never been called anything other than Victoria in her life. She's five years younger than me, making her thirty-one, yet she often forgets I'm the big sister. Victoria is married to Everett, an equally boorish man with impeccable manners and zero personality. But he's filthy rich and the only son in a long line of only sons whose ancestor was some bigwig in the signing of the Declaration of Independence, or came over on the *Mayflower*, I forget which. Everett represents exactly what Victoria sought in a mate—position, prestige, and money.

Second, Victoria and our mother, Francis Lowe Carter, are two peas in a pod, mirror images, and any other cliché that describes two people so much alike, they could be a scientific study. They have similar mannerisms, serve on various boards of charitable associations, and finish each other's sentences. Did I mention that they both sit in judgment of those who, in their prehistoric opinion, dare to venture from their *place*? That place being in a social circle that is not theirs. My mother comes from money, what was once called old money. In today's terms it's known as Bill Gates and Richard Branson money. Neither she, nor her father, nor her grandfather ever worked. Work was something somebody else did. Somebody was the doorman, bellman, and pool man.

Third, my father, Landon Philip Carter, retired three years ago as a named partner in the most prestigious law firm in the country. Until he retired, I could count on one hand the number of times I saw him not wearing a tie, his Windsor knot so tight I was surprised he could even swallow. Now, his Bermuda shorts are pressed and his matching polo shirt buttoned up to the first button regardless of the temperature. He's not quite as bad as my mother, but he doesn't socialize outside his circle either, which revolves around golf, personal investments, and vintage cars.

My job, as the firstborn in a long-legacy family, is to carry on the obligatory family name no matter that I was a girl. The name Lowe Carter has gotten me into more boys' gym classes, Boy Scout advertisements, and confused double takes than I care to admit. It never bothered me, because I preferred to play with the boys, but my mother would hear nothing of it. Her daughter, as she was, and her mother was before her, would be the perfect young lady. Unfortunately, I never got that DNA gene.

According to my mother, she is responsible for giving me life after enduring eighteen hours of hard labor before I entered the world screaming and demanding. She never said so, but she probably holds me responsible for her stretch marks, hemorrhoids, and sleepless nights while carrying me. I was constantly moving around like I had someplace important to go. I'm probably to blame for the fact that she leaks a little *down there* whenever she coughs or laughs too hard. She would absolutely never, ever discuss bladder control in polite company, or any company for that matter, but, when her eyes get big and the look of sheer terror covers her face, it's pretty evident what's going on below her beltline.

As tight as my mother is, I have a tough time picturing anything happening south of her trim waistline that would've produced me and my sister. I'm sure once my mother recovered from fainting at the sheer audacity of me even asking, she probably would have called it something akin to "wifely duties." Now I'm not married, never been a wife, and am certainly not a virgin, but I would never call the pure physical enjoyment of two people together a duty.

If not for the fact that I look exactly like my father, plus and minus a few critical anatomical appendages, I would swear I was adopted. Many times, in my youth, and, occasionally now that I'm a full-fledged adult, I prayed I was. The only thing I share with these people is a last name and the first eighteen years of my life at the same address in the largest house in Eagle Ridge Estates. I own my own business, much to the chagrin of my parents and my sister, and I have numerous friends who are considerate, kind, giving, and probably couldn't even spell the word pretentious. I volunteer at several homeless shelters, and I often drop a twenty into the torn paper cup of the woman who sits quietly on the corner near my building. I drive a twenty-year-old Toyota 4 Runner, not because I can't afford anything better, but because I love it. It's white with a tan interior and in immaculate condition. With regular maintenance according to the owner's manual and my favorite mechanic, she has over three hundred and fifty thousand miles on the odometer. I could walk into just about any car lot in America and pay cash for anything in their inventory, but driving a new car is not what I'm about.

I'm about common sense, existing on what I earn, honesty, and respect. I live in a normal-sized house in a modest subdivision, surrounded by minivans parked in the driveway because the garage is cluttered with bikes, skateboards, and treadmills. Jon, the fourteen-year-old who lives next door, keeps my pool clean and my yard mowed for twenty-five bucks a week. I could do it myself, and I did for many years, but Jon needed some responsibility. According to his mother Beth, while we were sitting on my patio drinking a beer, Jon needed to learn to earn money and not expect it to just be given to him. After a rough start, he's been doing a good job for the last year. Jon was supposed to keep an eye on my house while I was gone, but when he came over yesterday to get the key, I noticed a bright-red hickey on his neck. I gave the key to his mother instead.

However, I digress. The problem I earlier referred to is that I am the opposite of every member of my family. So, back to why I'm spending my precious free time in their company? At this point in my life, I have no fucking idea.

My parents live on a boat. Well, actually, it's a ship—a very large ship. At over seven hundred feet, the *Escape* is the largest private residence on the water. A combination of private yachting and luxury vacation home, she has one hundred and fifty-five luxury apartments. The ship has all the amenities of an upscale community, with shopping, restaurants, a health club, movie theater, medical facility, full-service laundry, two pools, nine Starbucks, and six Peet's Coffee locations. It has approximately three hundred crew members, including those working in the shops and businesses on board.

After construction began on the *Escape*, she was launched two years later with every unit sold. It's not a large ship, as cruise ships go, at just over forty-four thousand tons with a length of six hundred and sixty-two feet, and a beam, or width, of one hundred feet four inches. She has fifteen decks, not including the top deck, which contains a full-size tennis court, a pool, and a large patio all surrounded by a well-cushioned running track. Or, for the use of most of the residents, a walking track. Several of them are so wealthy they arrive and depart from the heliport on the stern of the main deck. The ship's top speed is twenty knots, or twenty-four miles per hour, but no one is in a hurry to get anywhere.

My parents' apartment is larger than my house. They have over four thousand square feet of plush, custom-designed, and decorated luxury. They live on deck fifteen, i.e. the deck just below the bridge, their huge living room filled with natural light and views of one hundred and eighty degrees; however, entering their apartment is like stepping into a sterile habitat. Everything is decorated in light colors, chrome, and glass so bright it hurts my eyes. The main living area features an open floor plan with a formal dining room, a piano that nobody plays, a library nook containing books nobody reads, and a large seating area. A leather couch with two side chairs face the windows looking out over the bow. Sliding glass doors, which I've never seen open, run the starboard side of the room. A rarely used kitchen with an oversized breakfast bar, and the master bedroom and bath is located on the opposite side. The veranda is about ten feet wide and runs across the front and side of the apartment, giving a spectacular view, if anyone cares to look at it. If this were my place, it would be completely different.

Each year, the residents plan the itinerary, including bringing on board expert guides and lecturers to prepare residents for each port they visit. Last year the *Escape* traveled to Antarctica, the Solomon Islands, East Asia, the western United States, Canada, and Alaska. This year, my part of their voyage consists of Australia and New Zealand. Every three or four days, the ship docks, and I leap at the chance to escape the judgmental looks of my parents and Victoria. I'm virtually guaranteed that my family will not accompany me on my excursions, Victoria and my mother preferring to spend their time in the spa or shopping, my father on the local golf course.

I love my parents and my sister, but I can tolerate them only in short bursts. We don't have much to talk about, and we stay away from controversial topics, which are most of them. We definitely have a don't-ask, don't-tell relationship, which is not applied equally to Victoria. They ask her about Everett, whom my parents adore, but never pose any questions about anyone I might be seeing. Currently, I'm in-between, as they say, so there's nothing to talk about, but that's not the point.

The flight from Phoenix to LAX to Sydney is at least eighteen hours long, give or take two or three for delays and whether the jet stream is in our favor. I treated myself to a seat in business class, where I could decompress over several glasses of free bourbon and one of the unread lesbian romances from the neat stack on my bookshelf at home. By the time I landed in Sydney, passed through customs, and caught a cab to the port, I had shifted my mindset to endure this trip.

## CHAPTER TWO

*Day One*
*Port of Sydney*

"Oh my god. Why did I volunteer to work the cleanup shift last night?" My sleep-deprived, scratchy voice filled my small cabin. Between the cold I've been fighting for a week, my early shift at The Club, and the typical confusion on board when we docked, it was going to be a very long day.

I hit the snooze button for the second time and rolled over. My head pounded, and I felt like I'd pulled the covers up just a few minutes ago, not several hours.

"Time to get up, Faith," my alarm said again. I slept like the dead and didn't hear a normal alarm clock, but if anyone said my name, I was instantly awake. I had found a clock that allowed me to record my own wake-up message and bought it immediately. When I knew it worked, I bought a second one for backup. It was out of my budget but well worth it.

My back hurt as I got out of bed. At twenty-six, I was too young to have back problems, so the fact that I'd been on my feet all day yesterday or needed a new mattress had caused them. Probably both, but unless I won the lottery, I couldn't do anything about either reason. My chances were zero, because as they say, "You can't win if you don't play." I work too damn hard for my money to piddle it away on a guaranteed loser. That, and it's a little difficult to buy a Powerball ticket in the middle of international waters.

I shuffled the few feet to the small bathroom in my cabin. Even though I was on the largest luxury ship in the world, I was the hired help, and my room in the "room and board included" was about the size of one in a small hotel. That was okay. I didn't need much—just a place to sleep, what little I did get. I have a bathroom and a small kitchenette, one matchbox closet, and a porthole just above the water line. Pictures of my mum and sister Angelica fill every surface, however few there are, and spill over onto the small fridge that usually contains Diet Coke and not much else. I eat most of my meals in the ship's restaurants or in the small crew galley on deck four.

As I stood under the hot water, I thought about how grateful I was to be only five feet, two inches tall. The shower is miniscule. I have no idea how Jeff, my neighbor, keeps himself clean. He's well over six feet tall and must weigh at least two hundred and forty pounds. I often hear him banging against our shared wall and, on more than one occasion, a few curse words.

I moved to cabin thirteen on deck five last year, when Jax, the crew member who had eight more days seniority than I did, quit. My previous one was smaller and didn't have a porthole. In the eight years I've called the *Escape* home, I've made countless friends from all over the world and picked up a few trinkets that give the gray walls and drab, institutional furniture of my home some life.

Knowing exactly how much hot water I had, I quickly scrubbed from aft to stern, carefully around the sensitive spots in the middle. I'd had another steamy dream with my faceless lover and had woken more than a little aroused. My mystery woman had been keeping my subconscious company for months, which was my body's way of telling me it needed a little attention. Judging by the aggressiveness and creativity of the woman in my head, I needed more than a little.

Dating residents was strictly forbidden, but we were all adults, and some could keep secrets better than others. However, I knew at least four crew members who'd been fired after their dallying with an owner was discovered. Each time somebody's big mouth had caused the problem, and each time the employee was escorted off the ship at the next port. I guess they had to find their own way home.

Dating other workers was frowned upon, not because of fraternization, but because when it went bad, and it always went bad, both parties, and sometimes all three parties were stuck in the same multistoried, encapsulated neighborhood. This situation didn't leave many opportunities to meet others or relieve pent-up sexual tension other than with locals in the ports we docked. Several of us take advantage of the friends-with-benefits solution, including myself once in a while, but I prefer to do my "unwinding" on shore. Unlike the staff on a traditional cruise ship, we had days off, and most of us departed the minute we docked. This life was not conducive to a relationship with anyone not on board.

When others with a similar economic hardship as mine may have joined the military as their way out and up, I boarded the *Escape*. The day after I turned eighteen, I'd excitedly hurried up the gang plank with just about everything I owned in my small suitcase and the bag slung across my back. What I didn't need on board, I left at home with my mum. I'd lucked into the job while I was waiting tables at a restaurant in Tampa when the *Escape* was in port. I'd passed the psychological testing, on-site interview, and background check, which wasn't hard to do because I had no life and no time to get into trouble.

Similar to a standard cruise-ship crew, we typically signed on for ten- to twelve-month assignments. Once we'd put in our time, we either renewed or we went home. I had chosen to re-sign every time. The job was good, mainly because I got to see places and meet people I never would otherwise.

We worked about fifty hours a week and had two days off. Rarely were they sequential, but that was all right with me. We weren't paid much, and I sent most of my salary home, so I picked up any extra hours I could as often as I could. The crew members were from countries like Lithuania, Romania, the Philippines, Sweden, and the US. We were allowed to use the ship's amenities and lived on decks three, four, and five. Decks six through fifteen contained resident apartments and places to eat, watch a movie, play cards, and various other activities to keep the residents occupied.

After tying my shoes, I checked myself in the mirror on the back of the door. My shorts were pressed, the logo of the *Escape* embroidered on my shirt just above my ample left breast. Along with unruly curly hair, I inherited my mother's cup size. My boobs aren't overly large, but my polo shirt pulled a little tight across them.

I hustled to The Club and clocked in just in time. It was quiet this morning, as it always was the day we docked. We were typically in country from one to four days, enabling the residents the opportunity to disembark and explore the local sites. They could always walk on the treadmill or work out in the gym while we were at sea.

To keep busy, I folded some towels and sanitized the equipment. Even though it was the evening shift's responsibility to tidy up before they locked up, I always give everything a good dose of disinfectant before my shift. Germs spread like a nasty rumor in confined spaces, and you couldn't get much more confined than on a ship in the middle of an ocean with no land in sight. If one person got a cold, it wasn't long before everyone had the sniffles and the line at the medical center was out the door.

Halfway through my shift, Mr. Blackwell came in with his warm, wide smile and infectious good mood. Mr. B, as he requested I call him, is eighty-four, with a ruddy complexion, a head of white hair, and thick black glasses. Mrs. B had been a quiet woman whom I rarely saw. They'd been residents only a few months when she had a heart attack in her sleep and passed away the next day. Mr. B would often wander into The Club first thing in the morning, and considering he wasn't much for using the equipment, I got the impression he was lonely. He'd bring his extra-large mug of coffee and we'd talk, or he'd just sit and gaze out the window, lost in his own thoughts.

"Good morning, Faith." He beamed when he saw me.

"Back at you, Mr. B. How was the card game last night?" Yesterday he'd informed me proudly that he'd secured a seat at the bridge table for the evening session.

"Excellent," he said excitedly. "I won fourteen dollars from the Graysons. My partner was Thomas Howard, and for a young guy, he was pretty good." Mr. B's idea of young was anyone under seventy.

"Better be careful, Mr. B. Don't want you gambling away your Social Security check."

With the cost of an apartment on the *Escape*, no one was living off their government stipend, no matter how much.

"Nonsense." He waved, his hand brushing off my fake concern. "It's all that funny money that goes to the charity." Each month residents chose a charity to donate their winnings to.

"Did you watch your episode of *Grace and Frankie*?"

I'd introduced Mr. B to the Netflix series starring Jane Fonda and Lily Tomlin a few weeks ago. He'd been lamenting about not having anything to watch on the tele, and I'd mentioned the series to him. The show focused on two women, best friends in their seventies whose husbands became lovers and ultimately divorced them. I thought the show was hysterical, with a great cast. Mr. B was instantly hooked and binge-watched the first season that weekend. We were halfway through season two, with each of us watching an episode sometime during the week, then talking about it when we saw each other. Mr. B was warm and witty and an interesting man to talk with. But he was, first and foremost, a resident, and I was always careful to maintain a respectable distance with him.

We chatted for an hour before he left to attend the nondenominational church service on deck eight. Mr. B joked that the only way he could keep track of the days of the week was to go to the services on Sunday.

My relief was Joanne, a petite blonde with more energy in her four-foot, eleven-inches body than I would ever have. No wonder she was the aerobics, Pilates, and yoga instructor, and I simply stood behind the front desk. We chatted for a few minutes before I headed up to the main deck to help wherever I was needed. I was scheduled for the lunch shift at Remington's so I had a few hours in between.

In our staff meeting last week we were told that the McConnells, Sturgeons, Cobalts, and the Carters would be having family joining them when we docked in Sydney. It was just like going to visit their grandma in Florida, except this grandma lived on a ship and could be in any country in the world.

I knew most of the regulars and family members, with the exception of the Carter children, who came to visit every year. Last year I'd had a bad case of the flu, the year before, my appendix removed, and the year before that I was on vacation. Barring any major catastrophe, I'd meet Lowe and Victoria this year. Mr. and Mrs. Carter didn't talk much about their daughters, at least not to the staff, and I hadn't heard anything from anyone else. The Carters were a bit stuffy, in my opinion, but that didn't matter.

Leaving the club, I took the stairs to the main deck to help with the on and off boarding of residents and guests. Arrival and departure day was confusing, especially in a busy port like Sydney. People were coming and going, looking for their tour groups, residents and guests were boarding, and departing and extra hands were always welcome. As I approached the area, I saw that the tour group had already departed, and that area of the deck was clear. I caught the deck supervisor's eye, and he waved me over.

The wood on the main deck reflected the light from its nightly polishing. I was always afraid I'd slip and fall and land ungracefully on my butt. Tall white columns jutted from the floor to support an open atrium, above where tables for cards and plenty of quiet, intimate areas for reading or conversation were available. Tasteful, yet safe, railings provided a stunning view of the main deck below. Brian, our pianist, was playing an unobtrusive, calming tune on the grand piano to my right. Fresh flowers filled tables. This deck, like all the resident decks, held all the amenities the ultra-rich had come to expect.

"Ian, need any help?" Ian Wick was barely five feet tall but commanded his deck like General George Patton. I admired his tenacity and work ethic, and he was fair and level-headed and clear in his expectations. Everyone liked working his deck.

"Thanks, Faith, but everything is running smoothly. For some reason, and I won't question what, everyone knew what they were supposed to do and where they were supposed to go today. I think we've had only a dozen questions instead of the normal hundred."

SHUT UP AND KISS ME

SHUT UP AND KISS ME

"You know you just cursed our departure," I said, half joking.

"Probably." Ian chuckled. "But I'm off duty at six." He tilted his head and touched the earpiece in his left ear. "It's Rob on deck twelve. He needs help in the Starbucks there."

"Tell him I'm on the way." What neighborhood wouldn't be complete with at least one Starbucks? We had one on each resident deck.

As I headed back toward the stairwell, I rounded the corner too sharply and collided with a firm, solid body. I stepped back, catching my breath and apologizing.

"Oh, my goodness, I'm so sorry. I—" Whatever else I was going to say stopped somewhere between my brain and my mouth. This wasn't a resident, but someone I'd never met before, and she was absolutely gorgeous. I would have remembered meeting her.

My heart skipped ahead a couple of beats, and my pulse kicked up—a lot. I was completely focused on her and didn't think I could form a coherent thought if I had to. She wasn't thin or lean or any of the other model-body perfect adjectives but carried a few extra pounds in all the right places. I like women with something to hang on to, lots of skin to touch, and the self-confidence to bear it all. Her eyes were the color of the sky outside, and we were so close I could see a dark circle around her pupils. She had a few lines around her eyes and across her forehead, telling me she was older than me and not ashamed to admit it. A pair of sunglasses was perched on top of her head, covering some of her very, very short blond hair.

Our eyes met, and I couldn't tear mine away, the spark of interest reciprocal. The deck shifted under my feet. Just as I was about to fall to my knees and beg this woman to have breakfast in bed with me, her expression changed, and one eyebrow quirked upward.

"Are you all right?" she asked, her voice husky and smooth.

The way she was looking me over with more than a little appreciation in her eyes wasn't doing anything for my jumbled thoughts and overloaded senses. Oh my, I thought. This was going to be interesting. I reminded myself to breathe, blink, and swallow. Somehow, I managed to say, "Yes, are you? I'm so sorry. I wasn't looking where I was going." I hoped I sounded coherent.

She gave me another once-over before stepping back and smiling. She had a dimple on her left cheek and a pale scar above the corner of her left eye.

"No, it was my fault. I was looking at this." She waved the paper in her hand. "I was already planning what excursions I want to take. I need to be more careful," she said, appearing chagrined.

It was my turn to conduct an inventory of the woman in front of me—purely for professional reasons, of course. If she were hurt, then the legal department of the *Escape* would have to get involved.

She was wearing shorts, and her tanned legs went all the way to the ground, as my Uncle Clark would say. They weren't muscular, but they looked strong enough to walk more than a few miles. Her thighs looked good enough to straddle, and I forced myself to banish that thought before moving on in my inspection. Jesus, I really needed to get laid, and soon. Her V-neck T-shirt was thick and sparkling white, contrasting nicely with her equally tanned arms. She had an expensive-looking briefcase slung over one shoulder.

"Ms. Carter," Ian said from behind me. "Welcome back."

The woman's eyes stayed on mine for a few seconds longer before she looked past me.

"Thank you, Ian. It's good to see you again," the woman said, her greeting warm.

This might be one of the mysterious Carter daughters. We had only one set of Carters on board, but it was a common name. Maybe this woman was married? If so, it would be to another woman.

"Excuse me again," I murmured, practically stumbling over my feet in my haste to get some breathing room between me and this walking, talking sex appeal.

My legs were weak, and I had to hold on to the handrail as I carefully navigated down the stairs. What had just happened? I'd seen beautiful women before, even met a few, but I had never gone completely gaga stupid over one. It might take a few minutes to unscramble my brain, but I did have enough sense to know this woman could be trouble. I didn't go looking for it and, because my job depended on it, stayed away from it. Something told me Ms. Carter might be my biggest challenge.

## Chapter Three

As I waited for the elevator to take me to up to deck fifteen and my parents' apartment, I thought about the woman who had almost knocked me off my feet a few minutes ago. I couldn't pinpoint what it was about her, but I instantly found her extraordinary. Her hair was dark and secured at the nape of her neck. Her skin was tan, and not from the artificial light. Her eyes were dark, and she wore very little makeup. She looked to be in her early twenties, and who needed makeup at that age? She spoke with a British accent and was sexy in a modest, unassuming way.

Sure, my body reacted like it does when there's a spark of mutual interest. My heartbeat quickened, which made my pulse run a little faster, and I had a small case of the excitement butterflies dancing in my nether regions. I'm not one for casual hookups, but I also don't need to know the extensive details of someone's life before I sleep with her. I admit that in college I had more than a few one-night flings, courtesy of Jack Daniels and no roommate. Now in my thirties, I think I'm somewhere between needing to know more than a woman's first name and less than her political and socioeconomic views or her position on global warming. If that's on the second date, great. If it's after five or six or even a dozen, that's fine too.

I'd occasionally had a vacation fling, which, when I thought about it, was some of the most enjoyable times I'd had both in and out of bed. It must have been something about never having to worry about running into her in the city, or, God forbid, she walked into one of my stores. The strong reaction I had to the woman on the main deck more than confirmed that I was more than a little behind in some individual attention and mind-blowing, roll-your-eyes-into-the-back-of-your-head sex. And I was going to be on the *Escape* for the next three weeks, which fit nicely into my middle ground.

I'd scope out the restaurant this evening, and if I didn't see her, maybe I'd run into her on my before-bed walk. If not, I'd make it a point to find her in the next few days. The ship was large but didn't have nearly as many passengers as a regular cruise ship, where finding one woman out of thousands would be difficult, if not impossible. This woman was either a resident or staff member, either one of which might be tricky in locating her. If she were visiting one of the residents, the likelihood of her spending any time away from her hosts to be with me was slim.

A soft, melodic voice announced we'd arrived at deck fifteen. The doors opened silently, and I stepped out, turned left, and headed down the long corridor. My luggage might or might not have beaten me to my parents' apartment, but I wasn't worried. After the obligatory security search, I'm sure they'd be delivered first, due to the fact that my parents owned one of the largest, most expensive units on the ship.

The plush carpet under my feet had an intricate pattern specifically designed to hide wear marks and spillage that might occur as the residents walked to and from their units. There were six units on this deck, three on either side of the corridor, with two at the bow, two at the stern, and two in the middle. Or, for those of us non-ship goers, the front, rear, and middle of the ship.

I followed fresh vacuum tracks to my parents' door. A bright, gleaming number four was displayed prominently in the center. I briefly considered swallowing one or two of the pills Charlotte had dropped in my hand at the airport. However tempted, I wasn't much into drugs, preferring to power through instead. I took a couple of deep breaths and pushed the doorbell.

"Lowe, sweetheart. It's so good to see you again," my mother said just after she opened the door. While she was taking a quick glance of me, I was doing the same of her. My mother believed a woman couldn't be too rich or too thin, and she was both. Her hair was perfectly coiffed, most likely from one of the three beauty salons on board, her fingernails freshly manicured, and her makeup as impeccable as always. Her camel-colored slacks were the perfect length, her sweater the perfect contrasting color. Do you get the picture—perfect? She reached out and hugged me, and if she had hugged me like a mother should, I would have felt her hip bones poke into me. We exchanged the obligatory welcome kisses without lips actually touching cheeks before she turned me loose and closed the door behind me.

"Come in," she said calmly. "Victoria arrived yesterday and came aboard first thing this morning." My mother's tone clearly implied that I should have flown in last night, stayed at an outrageously expensive hotel, and waited for the *Escape* to dock this morning. My sister doesn't work, and she can afford to fly anywhere, anytime. I, however, cannot. Even though I own my own business, I can't just leave without a thought. Sure, I have staff, but unlike the rest of the occupants of unit number four, I have additional responsibilities.

My parents' unit consists of three bedrooms, three and a half baths, a kitchen stocked with the latest appliances, and a combination of living, dining, and sitting area that anyone on board, or dry land for that matter, would envy. As I stepped into the large room, Victoria and our father were seated in a pair of matching wingback chairs facing a wide expanse of windows overlooking Sydney Harbor.

"Look who's here," my mother chirped, as if surprised I'd rung the bell.

My father stood, out of gentlemanly politeness, and welcomed me with his standard "Hello, Lowe." He was dressed in green golf pants with a monogrammed green-striped polo shirt. He didn't move to give me a hug or the impersonal air kiss like my mother or anything else to acknowledge that he hadn't seen me in over a year. My father wasn't one for showing emotion about anything unless it was the balance of his bank account or the number of strokes on his golf scorecard. I could never picture him and my mother caught up in the throes of marital passion necessary to produce two children. As an adult who enjoyed the carnal pleasures in life, I certainly couldn't see it now either.

"You're looking well, Father." My father, at seventy-two, was tan from hours on the golf course or hitting golf balls off the sundeck. His shock of white hair was its normal length, with a razor-straight part on the left. In all the years since I started paying attention, my father's hair has never changed. He had a standing appointment in the barber chair every four weeks whether he needed his hair cut or not.

"Lowe, it's about time you got here," my sister said, tottering over to me on ridiculously high-heeled sandals. Victoria was wearing what she'd once described as lounging pants, which, to me, looked like over-priced sweat pants. Her matching zip-up jacket clinched it for me. She too didn't bother with the physical aspects of greeting, preferring to look me over, but not nearly as clandestinely as our mother. I knew what was going through her head, and it sounded something like, *"My god. When will she let her hair grow? She looks like a man. And I've told her countless times how to lose the extra weight she's carrying. And those clothes. Her business must not be doing well, because obviously she can't afford decent clothes for this trip."*

Victoria smiled at me, the expression she practiced in the mirror and I'd seen her give dozens of people she really wasn't interested in. How I would love to say to her, *"I like my hair this way. I don't need to spend hundreds of dollars every six weeks lightening it to hide the gray. I am perfectly comfortable with the way my body looks, whereas you, on the other hand, little sister, are so thin you look almost emaciated. And for my clothes, they are perfectly acceptable for this trip, or any other for that matter. And yes, Victoria, my business is doing very well. Thank you for inquiring."*

But instead of saying what was on my mind, I returned the perfunctory greeting, inquiring about her husband and her various charities that kept her days occupied and her evenings in the spotlight. When the obligatory conversation died, we were all relieved by a knock on the door.

"I'll get it. It's probably my luggage." I grabbed at a reason to leave the awkward silence. After the porter deposited my suitcase in my suite, I tipped him generously, then took my time settling in. The room I always stay in, also known as Suite A, is just past the main foyer to the left. Through a small entry area is the bathroom, complete with an oversized Jacuzzi tub and shower big enough for at least five of my most intimate friends. Dual rain-shower heads and a bench along one side provide plenty of space to sit comfortably or shave my legs.

Tucked discreetly behind two wooden carved doors is a small washer and dryer. A large desk, complete with a ginormous Apple monitor and all the office supplies I could want, sits across from a huge walk-in closet almost as big as my entire bedroom at home.

Farther in the suite is a king-size Tempur-Pedic bed topped with a large white headboard, dresser, two nightstands, and a small seating area. The entire wall beside the bed fully opens onto a private patio with two lounge chairs and a bistro table. Suite B is similar, but a pair of French doors opens onto the main veranda. Unable to delay any longer, I closed the door behind me.

"Lowe, would you like a cocktail?" my mother asked sweetly.

I glanced at my watch. It was only twelve thirty. My body wasn't quite sure what time zone it was in, but I always tried to acclimate to local time as soon as I landed. "No, thank you. It's a little early for me." I'd long suspected my mother had a drinking problem, but I had never seen her drunk. She never slurred her words or became unsteady on her feet, but she always had a drink in her hand just after noon and one all evening. As I expected, my mother fixed herself one, having no problem drinking alone.

I made a few comments about changes in the decor: some new artwork, a different couch, and new patio furniture. I inquired about my mother's bridge club and my father's golf game. Their responses were predictable, and I learned nothing I didn't already know.

My mother glanced at her watch before she spoke. "You need to get cleaned up, Lowe. We'll be heading down to lunch shortly. We have reservations for one fifteen."

What my mother really meant was, *"Change your clothes. I don't want people to see my daughter dressed like that."*

Begrudgingly, I stood, but not before saying, "I won't be long."

And I wasn't. It didn't take more than three minutes to wash my face and hands, apply some lip gloss, and grab a light jacket. I stepped into the foyer where my family was waiting and was met with disapproving reactions. My mother's lips were pursed, Victoria's eyes were pinched, and my father was already safely in the corridor. I knew that with my mother's proper breeding and since Victoria had learned everything from her, they would never say a word. I don't think either one of them would say shit if they had a mouthful, but their disapproval was crystal clear to me.

My best friend Charlotte and I talked about my family and their quirks before and after every visit. The conversation always grew livelier as the beer bottles and shot glasses lined up on the bar. She thought I got a perverse joy in tormenting my mother and sister, and I'm not so sure she's wrong. I don't intentionally do things to irritate them or piss them off, but Victoria and my mother are two of the most ridiculous people I've ever seen. They pretend they live in nineteenth-century England, when I know they both have the latest iPhone, iPad, and *i* everything. They are all about appearances and position, whereas I look for substance and heart. They judge people by how much money they have and their station in life, I by their character.

We were silent as we walked down the corridor to the restaurant. In the center of decks nine through fourteen were two restaurants and a casual lounge. I'd eaten in every restaurant on the ship more than once, my parents dining out at least once a day. I've never seen my mother consult a recipe, let alone pick up a pot. Our cook always took care of such things. My parents didn't have a full-time cook on the *Escape,* just Margarete, who came in each afternoon to tidy up and prepare cocktails and light appetizers.

"Good afternoon, Robert." My mother greeted the host as we stepped inside the restaurant. The Remington was located two decks below my parents and was mid-sized and mid-priced, at least as it relates to other restaurants on the *Escape.* The lights were turned up, and the menu offered a variety of midday meals. In about four hours the lights would dim, the starched white tablecloths and linen napkins would appear, the wait staff would change, and the menu with no prices would replace the lunch one.

"Mrs. Carter. Good to see you again."

"These are my daughters, Victoria and Lowe." Even though my mother introduced us, she didn't identify who was who. She also didn't acknowledge the host's greeting. "They're staying with us for the next three weeks, so please put everything on our account." It wasn't a conversation. It was an order.

"Certainly, Mrs. Carter. If you'll follow me, your table is ready."

We walked through the dining room, and I took a quick glance at my fellow patrons, nodding at a few familiar faces, but not seeing the woman that had captured my attention when I boarded. We settled into our seats, my father sitting next to the window with my mother beside him, Victoria across from her, and I took the remaining chair. Our seating arrangement never changed. It enabled my mother and Victoria to talk about things they had in common, and the same with my father and me, without any cross-table confusion. Before we even had a chance to settle in, our server greeted us and asked for our drink orders. Not surprisingly, my mother asked for a gin and tonic, my sister a Manhattan, and my father a dry martini. When I looked up from my menu to give my order of a simple iced tea, my mind went blank.

Standing at the end of our table in a pristine-white, long-sleeve shirt, colorful blue-patterned tie, and a spotless black apron was the woman from downstairs. I'm sure I sat there with my mouth gaping open, and she was more put together than I was. She smiled politely, waiting for me to reply. She wasn't holding a pad or pencil. The wait staff in every restaurant had to be able to convey orders to the kitchen without the slightest error, regardless of the number of people seated around the table. We'd hardly exchanged a dozen words so far, but I was amazed at how much I was drawn to her.

"Lowe, she's waiting," Victoria said, clearly annoyed.

"Oh yes, sorry," I stammered. "Um…hello. I'll have an iced tea, please," I added.

"Would you like lemon and sweetener with it?"

"Yes, I would. Thank you, Faith," I responded, reading the name embroidered on her starched shirt, just above her left breast. I had to drag my eyes away so as not to be impolite. Something in her eyes flared for a moment and then was instantly gone. It was so fast I wasn't sure it was ever even there. No one else at the table would've seen it, since they all had their faces buried in their menus. They had never looked up at Faith when she arrived.

I watched her stop at an adjacent table to check on a large, boisterous group finishing their dessert. I don't mean to sound like a pig, but Faith looked just as good walking away as she did from the front.

"Lowe, what are you staring at?" My mother's voice was harsh.

"What?"

"I asked you what you are staring at so rudely."

"Nothing. Just looking around and recognizing a few familiar faces." It was a lie. However, the disapproval on my mother face told me it wasn't a very good one.

I eagerly waited for Faith to return, and my heart kicked up when I saw her round the corner carrying a tray with our drinks.

As she approached our table, she looked at everyone except me. She named off the drinks and set them down in front of each one of us, saving mine for last. My family didn't look up or even acknowledge her, which irritated the hell out of me. But it always had. They had a way of keeping the hired help in their place simply by ignoring them. I wasn't like that, and when Faith finally looked at me, I thanked her. Her eyebrows rose slightly, just enough to show that my greeting had surprised her.

"Have you decided on your choice for lunch today?" Her voice was smooth and melodious, her accent captivating. My mother rattled off her order, changing just about everything. My sister followed suit, and my father simply ordered a filet, rare, and a baked potato. When Faith turned her attention to me, the little wobble in my stomach teetered again. I couldn't remember the last time I'd been so physically affected by someone I'd just met. And technically we hadn't even done that.

I placed my order, thanked Faith again, and watched her disappear around the corner after handing our menus to the host as he passed.

"How are your stores doing, Lowe?" my father asked, barely glancing at me.

In his mind, my pack-and-ship franchises were nothing compared to Victoria's husband's family, who owned one hundred and eighty-two auto dealerships across the country.

"Really well," I answered, tamping down my pride in my success. He wouldn't notice or care. "Sales are up four hundred and twenty percent year over year. I've expanded into a few adjacent spaces, which increased my PO boxes by sixty percent, giving me more long-term cash flow."

"Excellent," he said. "What are your margin and your earnings?"

I recited the figures that represented the very positive financial picture of my business. Again, the only language that really mattered in his world.

He nodded his approval and asked, "And your plans for expansion?"

Not "are you going to expand?" It was all about growth and quantity with him.

"I'm not sure yet," I said, my response guarded. My father had a way of making me feel like I had to defend my lack of empire building.

"I'm looking for additional opportunities, but nothing has been right." That was partially true. He didn't need to know I didn't spend every spare minute trying to become the largest franchisee in the country. I worked hard, but I did have a life—one that I enjoyed immensely. Adding more stores would seriously cut into my spare time. I made a good living with what I had. It paid my bills, I could buy almost anything I wanted, and I was building my retirement.

"Charles informed me you haven't touched your trust fund. You need to use those funds for your future growth."

My maternal grandmother had left me a large amount of money when she died a decade earlier. I hadn't spent a penny of it and wasn't going to. I'd left it where it was and now regretted it. It was time to move it to my financial planner and out from under the roots of the family tree, so to speak.

"Charles has no business talking to you about *my* account." It had been solely in my name for over ten years.

"Charles has been handling our finances for more than forty years. He's almost like family," my father replied, his tone indignant.

"I don't care if he's my long-lost brother," I said, unsuccessfully trying to keep the anger from my voice. "He has a duty of confidentiality, and he's breaching that if he's talking to you."

"That is too much money to act so flippant about," he said as if scolding me.

"I'm not flippant about it. I take it very seriously. But what I do, or don't do with it, is my business," I said again.

A tall thin man in his forties stopped at our table, saving me from my father's additional opinion and lecture regarding what he obviously thought was my fiscal irresponsibility.

After introductions and several minutes of polite, neighborly chitchat, he returned to his table. My mother informed us that he was a new resident on their deck. With obvious distaste, she told me that he'd sold his start-up company to Google for $735 million. New money wasn't the same as old in her book.

I'd heard of the man's company and used one of his applications in my store. Of course, I didn't dare mention that I'd invested in his little start-up and had reaped a significant financial benefit from the sale.

"Landon, I wish you wouldn't talk business at the table," my mother complained, implying that we were discussing an unmentionable bodily function.

"When else am I going to do it? We don't see her any other time."

Here we go again, I thought. I was wondering how long it would be before one or both of them pulled the visiting guilt card out of the drawer.

"How long has it been, Lowe?" Victoria asked, piling on in her squeaky voice.

I didn't answer. She knew damn good and well the date of my last visit.

"I own a business." It was the same reason I'd used for years. "I can't just up and leave anytime I want. Not to mention the cost to travel to wherever you are." I shifted my gaze from Victoria to my parents. The look on my father's face told me that was not a smart thing to say. This was the same tired argument we had every time we got together.

"You know, planes fly both ways," I said for the first time. I was fed up with being held to a double standard.

My mother shot me daggers, while Victoria sat back and waited for the fireworks. It didn't take long.

"Don't speak to your mother like that," my father said quietly yet effectively.

"I'm not being disrespectful. I'm just stating a fact. You two are retired and have more money than God. Nothing's stopping you from visiting me."

"In Arizona?" My mother asked the question like we still had outdoor toilets and Indians roaming the dusty streets.

"Yes, Mother. Phoenix is the fifth largest city in the country. We have outstanding museums, the arts, five-star resorts, and fabulous places to eat." My mother wore an expression that said she'd rather go to Walmart than to where I lived. When did she get like this? Or had I just noticed?

Faith approached, our meals on a large round serving platter discouraging any future conversation on this topic. At least until she was out of earshot. One never talked about family issues in front of the help.

❖

My hands were shaking as I picked up the plates from under the warming lights. I hadn't allowed myself to think about the woman at table six until I sent the meal to the kitchen. I took a moment to gather my thoughts and pull myself together. So, she was definitely one of the Carter girls. However, girl wasn't really the right word.

She was a grown woman and, most definitely, a lesbian, and her name was Lowe. What an interesting name, but then again, she looked like an equally interesting woman. I knew there was more than a slight chance I'd run into her again. I wasn't sure if that was a good thing.

Lowe Carter was nothing like her other family members at the table. They barely paid any attention to me when I interacted with them, whatever job I had. I wondered how long I could stand at the end of their table before they even acknowledged my presence this afternoon. But not Lowe. She did more than say hello. She actually looked at me, and her greeting had turned from polite to appraising to indicating definite interest.

I don't think I'm beautiful, but a few heads have turned my way over the years. Yet I have to admit my reaction to the look in Lowe's eyes was totally unexpected. It took my breath away. They were so expressive I wanted to crawl inside and disappear into their mystery. It was obvious she was interested, but I had found long ago that first impressions can be very wrong and short-lived. However, that's usually the first thing I notice about someone—their eyes. I took a deep breath and exited into the dining room.

I sensed tension at the table when I returned with their lunch. Nothing was said as I placed the orders on the table in front of the family. I didn't bother to look at Lowe's parents or sister. What was the point? I did, however, glance at Lowe and had the same reaction I'd had the other times I saw her. My stomach fluttered, and I imagined things I shouldn't be thinking about when carrying plates of hot food. After getting everything settled, I felt Lowe's eyes on me as I walked away. I had to focus so I wouldn't stumble.

I wasn't any more or any less attentive to their table than I was with any others in my section, but I was so aware of being in the same room with Lowe I almost overfilled the coffee cup at table twelve.

My relief tapped me on my shoulder, and I jumped.

"Sorry, Faith. I thought you heard me."

I was standing in front of the prep counter in the kitchen daydreaming about Lowe.

"Sorry, Barb. What did you say?"

"I said things have slowed down, so let's hand off."

Barb was referring to the process we went through as we transitioned the servicing of our tables to the next shift. It took ten minutes to make the rounds of my tables, saving the Carters' for last. They were just finishing their meal and barely acknowledged Barb and me. To them, one server was the same as another. The very visible exception was Lowe. I hustled away, leaving Barb to close them out, and was just about to push open the door to the back room, when I heard my name. I turned around and looked up into the bright-blue eyes of Lowe Carter.

"I want to apologize for my family's rude behavior," she said, nodding in their direction.

Standing in front of Lowe I realized she was quite a bit taller than me. Flashing on the anticipation of her slowly leaning down to kiss me, I felt a little dizzy and had to stop myself from swaying towards her.

"I'm sorry," I said. "I don't know what you're talking about." I was lying.

"Please," Lowe said, rolling her eyes. "They're rude, boorish, and ill behaved."

"Then why are *you* apologizing for them?" She seemed to be taken aback by my question.

"Because I don't want you to think I'm like them."

"It really doesn't matter what I think, Ms. Carter. Your parents are residents on the *Escape*."

"But that doesn't give them the right to be rude. And what you think matters to me."

Lowe looked like she'd just stepped off a cliff into a dark abyss.

"That's kind of you Ms. Carter, but—"

"Please, call me Lowe."

"That's kind of you," I said, resisting the familiarity she'd granted me. It would help me to maintain distance. "But not necessary."

"Would you have coffee with me?" Lowe asked suddenly, looking surprised that she had. "Please. It'll be my chance to atone for my parents."

"Atone?" I felt several pairs of eyes on us. Lowe chuckled, and my mouth went dry while other parts got wet.

"The best I can come up with at the spur of the moment," she said sheepishly, and my stomach fluttered.

"Would you have used a more practiced line otherwise?"

"No. I don't use lines," Lowe said simply.

I looked at her for a long moment before saying something equally surprising. "No, I don't believe you would." How I knew that was a mystery. Wishful thinking? Gut instinct, maybe? "I'll be free in about ten minutes."

Lowe's smile lit up her face. "Meet you at The Cuppa?" Lowe asked, referring to the coffee shop one deck up.

Lowe wouldn't make a good poker player, her expression saying it all. I, however, had learned to disguise my emotions. At least outwardly.

"Make it twenty."

## CHAPTER FOUR

I ran. No way in hell was I was going to sit across from Lowe Carter smelling like food. My cabin was on the opposite side of the ship and down at least half a dozen flights of stairs. I was naked before I hit the shower, which is not difficult because of the size of my place. In one minute, I was soaking wet and completely dry five minutes later. Luckily, I'd done my laundry yesterday, so my favorite, most flattering jeans were hanging in my tiny closet, along with the dark-brown, capped-sleeve T-shirt that brought out the color of my eyes. My hair was still a little damp, so I pulled it up on top of my head and clamped it in place with a large clip. A little mascara, lip gloss, and I had six minutes to get to The Cuppa.

The coffee shop was on deck eight just outside the movie theater. It was built like any other coffee shop/café, with a large front counter flanking the far wall with several high-top tables with stools featuring thick-cushioned seats. Six other tables sat against the large floor-to-ceiling windows. The Cuppa served breakfast and lunch and had a display case of yummy snacks and treats, which I had a hard time staying away from.

With ninety seconds to spare I used the time to catch my breath before I met Lowe. I approached from the side and saw her sitting at a table for two on the outside patio. She was angled away from me, and I was able to study her for a few moments. She had a strong profile, the muscles in her jaw working as if she was chewing a piece of gum. She was wearing sunglasses against the midday glare, and I was glad I'd thought to grab mine as I ran out the door. She was drumming her fingers rhythmically on the table top. Was she inpatient for me to arrive? A girl could wish.

She must've sensed me watching her because she suddenly turned my way. She stood, pulled off her sunglasses, and motioned me over. She even held my chair as I sat down, which I found gallant and charming. The sun was warm on my back, a light breeze blowing my hair.

"Right on time," she said, sitting beside me, hiding her eyes behind her Ray-Bans.

"You sound surprised." I was glad my voice didn't betray my nerves.

"In my experience, when a woman says twenty minutes, she means thirty or forty."

"I could go away and stand over there if you'd like?" I said, teasing, and pointed to a potted plant on the other side of the patio.

"No. Absolutely not necessary." Lowe smiled. "It's refreshing, and I'll keep that in mind about you. What would you like?"

"Just a plain black coffee." She looked at me, evidently surprised. "What?"

"No caramel, macchiato, double latte, sweet, no-fat, extra whip?"

"No. Just plain black coffee."

"You're a woman after my own heart." She put her hand over her heart.

I almost mimicked her action, but I would've done it to stop mine from hammering out of my chest.

"Not hardly. I just have plain, simple tastes."

"I don't mean to sound like a cliché, but I don't see anything plain or simple about you."

"You don't even know me."

"Then I'll get our coffee and we'll start to remedy that situation. Hold my seat. I'll be right back."

Lowe hurried to the counter and placed our order, then turned around and smiled at me again. I was glad I was sitting down because I got all tingly all over this time. She'd replaced her white T-shirt with a bright-red tank top, and the color suited her. The counter wasn't busy, and it didn't take long before she returned with two cups of coffee covered with bright-green lids.

"My turn to serve you," she said, setting the cup on the table in front of me.

"And you're doing a wonderful job."

"Thanks, but I don't think I could manage much more than this." She grabbed a sugar packet and shook it.

"Oh, I don't know. You look pretty capable to me." I couldn't resist giving her a once-over, liking what I saw.

"Thanks, but I don't know how you do it. Especially with people like my parents." She poured the packet into her cup and stirred it with a thin yellow straw.

"Practice." Unfortunately, my response was far too true.

"I just don't get it." Lowe frowned, leaned back in her chair, and blew on her coffee to cool it. "I wonder if they were always like that or if I just noticed?"

"Does it matter?" It didn't to me. It was my job, and with it came the good and the bad. I sipped my coffee, the hot liquid almost burning my tongue. I took off the lid to let some of the heat escape.

"Not that I have to experience it much, since I only see them once a year. But they are my family, and I don't want people to think I'm like them."

"That's twice you've said that. Do you socialize with the same people?"

Lowe laughed, a sound like a melodic wind chime.

"Oh, right. That was a stupid question," I said like a dummy. "They live here." I raised my hands, palms up, indicating our current real estate.

"It wasn't a stupid question."

I knew otherwise. "Where do you live?" A stray few hairs tickled my face, so I brushed them back.

"Phoenix."

"Arizona?" Lowe nodded as she sipped her coffee. "I've never been to Arizona."

"Well, I've never been to Sydney, so I guess that makes us even. Where are you from?"

"Originally, Ipswich. It's a little town in Suffolk, England."

"Where is that relative to London?"

"About sixty miles northeast."

"Big city? Small town?"

"Small town. I think in the last census it had around a hundred and fifty thousand people."

My hometown had been one of the most important docks in English history. Today, it primarily stored dry bulk goods and all types of shipping containers, and it had slips for two hundred private boats at the Haven Marina. The *Escape* had docked in Ipswich after I hired on.

"I spent some time in Northampton."

"When?" Northampton is about the size of Ipswich, located approximately seventy miles northwest of London.

"I was in high school. My parents thought it would be good for me to perform some type of community service."

"To give back?"

"No. To look good on my college applications," Lowe said with a hint of sarcasm.

I let that comment pass. "How did you like it?"

"Loved it. Actually, more than I thought I would. I went back three more times during the summers. Because of that experience, I give my employees sixteen hours of paid time off for volunteer work every year."

"Really? What do you do?"

"Nothing sexy or glamorous, I'm afraid. I own some pack-and-ship franchises."

"I love those places," I said honestly. "There was one near my house growing up, and they had coldest soda machine."

"In Ipswich?" It was Lowe's turn to be stunned.

"No. I lived in Tampa for many years. My friends and I would stop on the way home from school. It was so hot, and they had a big red soda machine inside. I'd hold a can to the back of my neck to cool off. The owner, this guy named Mr. Samuels, was the nicest man. His wife would bake cookies and leave a tray on the counter."

"Sounds like good memories," Lowe said.

It was, only when I found enough money on the sidewalk to buy a can. We couldn't afford seventy-five cents, but I didn't tell Lowe that.

"How did you get to Tampa?"

"My father came over on a work visa when I was ten." Then ran off, leaving me and my mother to fend for ourselves. We'd moved to Tampa when my mum married Nathaniel. I didn't bring that detail up either. Too much baggage on the first date is not good. Wait. This was not a date.

"Is your family still in Tampa?"

"Yes. My mother and little sister."

"Do you get to see them often?" Lowe asked, stirring her coffee again.

"Once or twice a year. I take my vacations there and try to get back for a long weekend if we're nearby. How long have you been in the pack-and-ship business?" I changed the subject, not wanting to talk about myself too much.

"Fourteen years."

"That's impressive," I commented honestly. My coffee was finally at a temperature level that I could drink it.

"My father doesn't think so."

"Oh, sorry," I said as quickly as the smile fell from her face. "I didn't mean to hit a nerve."

"No. That's all right. He was criticizing me earlier because I haven't expanded again."

"Again? How many stores do you have?"

"Twenty-four."

"Twenty-four?" I asked, incredulous and impressed. "How many does he think you should have?"

"As many as I can. Size matters to him."

I chose to ignore that analogy. "How many employees do you have?"

"A hundred and thirty-eight."

"Twenty-four stores and a hundred and thirty-eight employees? You're practically the next FedEx." She smiled again. I'd have to think of other things to say to see her do that again.

"Not hardly, but I enjoy it. Any less and I'd be bored. Any more and I'd be too busy to spend my vacation on a ship with rude, irritating parents, a pretentious, obnoxious sister, and a beautiful woman sitting across from me on my first day."

My stomach fluttered at her compliment. I told it to behave because the flattery came out of her mouth too smoothly. "Then why do you?"

Lowe looked at me, but I couldn't see her eyes clearly through her dark sunglasses. "Because it's the right thing to do," she said simply.

"The right thing?"

"Yes. They're family, whether or not I like it, and I was raised that family is number one."

I nodded. I knew what she meant.

"So, you grin and bear it?"

"In a manner of speaking, I suppose."

Lowe gazed across the stern out to the water of Sydney Harbor. She was very attractive in a handsome, almost androgynous way, and I was more than a little attracted to her. I needed to be careful.

"Are you happy doing what you're doing?"

"Sitting here with you? Yes."

"No. I meant with your life."

Lowe was quiet for so long I thought I'd overstepped.

"Yes."

"Then I don't see a problem. But again, you've known me less than thirty minutes, so my opinion should not be the one to listen to." My comment was a success, because Lowe smiled again.

"What are you doing the rest of your life, Faith? I need to have you beside me, especially when I visit my parents."

I choked on my coffee that suddenly went down the wrong way. In some other place and time that remark would've made a pretty good proposal. But this was here and now. Lowe patted me hard on the back.

"Are you okay?"

I nodded and signaled her to give me a minute to recover.

"Sorry. I'm fine." I coughed a few more times, clearing my lungs. "Just went down the wrong tube, I think." I wiped tears from my eyes with a brown, scratchy napkin I tugged from the holder.

We sat there not talking for a few minutes, both of us apparently comfortable with our own thoughts. It was nice, and I didn't feel any pressure to fill the silence. After a few more minutes Lowe asked, "How long have you been on the *Escape*?"

"Eight years."

"Wow. That's a long time, isn't it?"

"Actually, yes. I'm one of the longest tenured staff."

"Congratulations," Lowe said, and I felt she meant it. "I've been visiting my parents for four years, and I know I would've remembered seeing you before," she said, looking me over again.

"I work all over the ship. I was probably everywhere you weren't." Lowe gazed at me for so long I wanted to fidget.

"That's a shame. I would have enjoyed spending time with you."

The subtle meaning under Lowe's words was clear, and my stomach ricocheted against my ribs. I was acutely aware of a low throb in my girl parts.

"I have to go," I said abruptly, stumbling out of my chair. My body was saying something very different, and I was more than a little tempted to listen to it for once. Yet as much as I might want to be the recipient of a fling with Lowe Carter, I needed this job. I'd probably just lost it from my errant thoughts and lose tongue.

"Thank you for the coffee." I looked at her wet lips and almost changed my mind.

## Chapter Five

Holy mamma mia! What just happened? Did I miss a part of the conversation? How did my invitation for an innocent cup of coffee turn into what? Seduction? Promise? Potential? I know I was probably suffering from jet lag and seriously needed a nap, but my attraction to Faith clobbered me out of left field.

I replayed our conversation and what I did or might have said to make her bolt like I was on fire. Could it have been because I couldn't keep my eyes off her? Did she hear my heart pounding so loud it even scared me? Did she sense my almost constant state of arousal since...Jesus, was it only this morning? Could she read my mind to know what I want to do with her, to her? Did I have a flashing sign that said I want to touch you blinking over my head?

Whatever it was, I'd better rein it in if I wanted to see her again. Wait, did she want to see me again? My brain was just as twisted as my insides. What in the hell was going on? I've been with women since I was seventeen, and none of them had me as tied up as Faith had in just a few hours.

I shifted my thoughts to consider if I'd forgotten to do anything the last few days while getting everything ready for this trip. I'm pretty good at that, especially when it comes to my job. When I step into one of my stores, I'm all business. I have three general managers for my fourteen stores in Arizona, one to manage the seven locations in San Diego, and the third for the three in Las Cruces,

New Mexico. A week ago I drove to Tucson and terminated one of my managers. I fired his sorry ass for inappropriate behavior with two of his employees. For God's sake, does he not watch the news? If he does, he's stupid. If he doesn't, he's even stupider. Either way, I enjoyed every minute.

When the complaint first came to my attention, I hired an independent firm to investigate. Even though I believed the women, the man was innocent until proven guilty. My already short patience was even shorter as I waited for the process to be completed. I was briefed by the investigator at 8:50 am, and the inappropriate manager was unemployed by noon. I spent the rest of the afternoon in a meeting with the two employees who had filed the original complaint, left the store around six, and checked into the Hilton not far from the University of Arizona campus.

I was unwinding from the day when the waitress brought me my second Crown and Coke and chatted me up. She was floating all the signs that she'd like to "talk" more, but I already had plans for the night. Her name was Suzanne.

Suzanne is a single mother of four-year-old twins I met two years ago when I was in town. I literally ran into her with my grocery cart and invited her for a cup of coffee to apologize. I was opening my first store and was in town for weeks keeping an eye on the construction. After several dates, Suzanne got her mother to babysit, and we burned up the sheets in my hotel. I called her every time I was in town, and we met up more times than not. That night would be one of those. I could've easily driven back to Phoenix and slept in my own bed, but why should I sleep alone when I could have charming company?

The thundering sound from the stack horn brought me back from my memories of the night with Suzanne, and thoughts of potential nights with Faith took their place. I'm not a player, but I appreciate women, and if we both are looking for the same thing, then there's no harm. I know others feel differently about sex, and that's fine with me.

I got up just after the second belching of the horn. We were about to depart, and the traditional three blasts signaled the ship was pulling away from the dock. I took the stairs to the top deck and found an empty place next to the railing. It wasn't difficult. The *Escape* leaving port was not like your traditional cruise ship, where guests crowded along the starboard-side rails waving to those who had dropped them off or the throngs of people who just simply like to see a monster ship move slowly through the water.

I stood there for quite some time watching the harbor and the Sydney skyline disappear into the distance. It was hard to believe that less than twenty-fours ago I was bundled up under a blanket in my living room watching the evening news. The temperature today in Sydney was supposed to be eighty degrees. I did some quick math in my head and corrected that forecast to twenty-six degrees Celsius. Better get started on thinking in metric now.

I found my parents sitting in the main room, each holding their traditional before-dinner cocktail. My sister stood beside them, clutching a glass of white wine, her perfectly manicured red nails a sharp contrast.

"Margarete can fix you a cocktail," my mother said, vaguely pointing in the direction of the small, compactly packed bar not far from where they were sitting. I hadn't seen Margarete, their cook and housekeeper, when I came in, and I wasn't going to make her leave whatever she was doing, walk all the way across the apartment, and fix it for me. Good grief. I was perfectly capable of making my own drink.

"I'll get it. No need to bother her," I said, dropping three ice cubes into a thick tumbler.

"That's her job," Victoria said like I hadn't read her job description.

"I know." I poured liberally and put the top back on the decanter. "But I can get my own drink."

Victoria tsked. "Lowe, you have to let them do their job," she said, like I was demeaning myself by doing it.

I didn't like Victoria's choice of words. "It's fine, Victoria. I even wash my own sheets at home."

I loved sticking it to my pretentious, stuck-up sister. I did it to make a point, which, more often than not, sailed over her head and sometimes just to see that sour pout on her face and make her stomach churn. This time she shook her head as she tsked.

"We expected you earlier," my mother said. Translation— *where were you? You know cocktails are at six thirty, followed by dinner at seven.*

"Just getting some sun and watching the departure." Victoria looked at me like I was little more than a common tourist. "It was warm, and the skyline was more beautiful than what I'd seen in pictures." I took a large swallow of my cocktail. Since I'd made it heavy on the Crown and light on the Coke, my throat burned as the warm liquid slid down and settled in my stomach.

I paid half attention to what my sister and mother were talking about, my father adding a word or two now and then. I was thinking about Faith and our short, but oh so interesting conversation. What must her life be like living here surrounded by all this luxury and pretentiousness? It was certainly different than my parents' as they cruised from port to port doing I have no idea what. Faith, on the other hand, had to work and put up with them.

I hurried and cleaned up and changed into something my parents would find somewhat acceptable for dinner. I wasn't up to dodging the disapproving looks of both my mother and Victoria tonight. One or the other I can handle, but as tired as I was, enduring the two of them would be difficult.

During dinner, I constantly looked for Faith as either a server or a diner. Not seeing her, I let my mind wander to obscure things like how many countries Faith had visited. How many passports had she been through? What did she do for vacation? Were her friends other members of the crew? What did she do when she got sick? Did her family get to visit? Did she have to pay the outrageous prices for a haircut in the ship salon or for a massage? Did she get an employee discount? Was she involved with someone? These and a dozen other questions sprang to mind throughout the main course.

I'd barely kept up my end of the conversation, and Victoria kept shooting me daggers when I asked one of them to repeat the question or was caught obviously not paying attention.

"What is wrong with you?" she asked when my mother excused herself and headed in the direction of the ladies' room before the after-dinner cordials arrived. "You've been nothing short of rude all evening." She liked to chastise me.

I bristled at not only her tone but her audacity. She was far short of perfect herself. "I'm tired, Victoria," I said, the fib convenient. "I've been up for I don't know how many hours and time zones. I'm sorry if I'm not the perfectly mannered dinner companion." My father glanced between Victoria and me but wisely kept his mouth shut. I placed my folded napkin on the table in front of me. "Please tell Mother I'm going for a walk. Don't wait up," I said to anyone at the table who cared.

# Chapter Six

The gym was empty, as it always was at eight thirty in the evening. The mornings were filled with yoga and Pilates classes, and the early birds getting their miles in on the treadmill before lunch. During the afternoon, stragglers came in every now and then, but after four it was typically just staff. After all, it wasn't as if the residents would stop by on their way home from work.

Today was leg day. I did cardio every day but rotated working my arms and legs. This gave my muscles a chance to rest but also kept me in the gym every day without getting bored. I hit the leg press after my fifteen-minute warm-up, earbud snugly in place. I was learning French or, I should say, trying to learn French, with the help of Rosetta Stone. If we'd stayed in England I would have learned several languages, but I was making up for the lost opportunity now. We have a resident, Mr. Tillman, who is from Paris, and I practice every time I see him. The first time he ordered dinner in his native tongue, he laughed when I repeated it back to him in English. I got most of it right, but the oatmeal instead of potatoes would've been a surprise.

I was well into my routine, which included saying my lesson out loud, when I heard a voice behind me. I always have one earbud out for just this reason. I don't want to be caught unaware of my surrounding.

"No. I'll have tea instead." I turned around and was surprised to see Lowe, a towel in her hand, grinning at me. She'd obviously heard me ask my fictitious guest if they'd like coffee.

"I'll bring your tea right out. Will there be anything else?" I asked in French.

"No, thank you," she replied, continuing in the same language.

Lowe was wearing a pair of bright-red spandex shorts and a red-and-white racer-back tank top, both of which fit as tight as any one-piece swimsuit would. Her hair was tousled, and her cross-trainer shoes looked well used. I couldn't believe this was the fourth time I'd seen her today.

"Your accent is really good,"

"Thanks. As is yours."

"Twelve years of French lessons from Madame Phillipe. She said I always butchered a beautiful language. I think she was just an old crab."

I laughed at Lowe's description of her French tutor. "I've been learning only a few weeks, so I'm no expert."

"May I?" she asked, indicating the open equipment. "I don't want to intrude."

"No, no problem," I said, glad she was going to stay. "Do you have a lot of opportunity to speak the language? Do you spend time in France?" The closest I'd ever been was when we docked in Paris, and Mr. Tillman of course.

"My mother made my sister and me spend a month in Paris every summer." She adjusted the weight settings on the lat pull-down bar. "She thought it would instill a genteel nature," she added, screwing up her face as if simply saying the words was distasteful.

"And did it?" I slapped my hand over my mouth. "Oh my god, that didn't come out right. What I meant was—"

"It's okay. I know what you meant." Lowe waved her hand, dismissing my faux pas. "I know how to carry on a conversation when it's boring as hell, what fork to use, and how to compliment something when I hate it. But I don't live and breathe good manners like my mother and sister."

I watched her slip a pair of weight-lifting gloves on her hands. Earlier this afternoon I'd noticed she had long fingers and had allowed myself a short fantasy imagining them caressing me.

"They take it to the extreme, I'm afraid. And when the two of them are together...Don't get me wrong, I love my parents and sister, but there's a reason we grow up and move out. I'm sure my mother would like it if we got together more often, but I can take only so much."

Lowe completed several sets on the machine before moving to the next. I thought it sad that she wasn't close to her family. I loved my mother and sister and missed them terribly, and I'd spend more time with them if I could.

"What does your sister do?" I asked in between sets of hamstring stretches.

"Spend her husband's money and rule over the charities she's involved with."

Ouch, I thought. That's harsh.

"But she does good work, I suppose," she added. "She's on the board for the local children's hospital, the cancer center, and something else I don't remember."

"What's so funny?" I asked when she chuckled and shook her head.

"I can't figure out why someone as self-centered and narcissistic as Victoria would give her time to anything else."

I didn't answer. It was obviously a rhetorical question.

"I guess it's her idea of what a good society woman does." Lowe shook her head as if banishing the thought. "Enough about my dysfunctional family. What about yours?"

"Nothing so exciting or dramatic, I'm afraid," I said honestly.

"There's something to be said about normalcy. Come on. Spill." She used her hands to indicate I should do just that. "I shared with you, so it's your turn."

I filled Lowe in on the brief outline of my family tree as we finished our workout. More than once I caught her looking at me, as in "looking at me," her interest obvious. I reacted as anyone would but knew our mutual attraction couldn't go anywhere. I preferred not to make either of us uncomfortable, so I simply pretended I didn't see it.

Somewhere just past the halfway point of my routine, Lowe started speaking to me in French. She corrected a few of my words and pronunciation, and by the time we finished, I was speaking fairly well.

"I've got to run," I said reluctantly. I wanted to stay and talk with her more but knew better. Before she had a chance to respond, I said, "Enjoy the rest of your evening, and thanks for the French lesson."

Lowe's genteel training must have kicked in because she let me go without trying to persuade me otherwise.

I hurried down the hall and down the stairs to my cabin, disappointed she hadn't tried.

## Chapter Seven

I jumped on the treadmill as Faith walked away from me. Was I losing my touch? I'd given her every signal in my arsenal, and she didn't bite.

I ran a few miles to release my frustration as well as erase the image of firm, tan legs, bare arms, and sweat from my brain. Yeah, right. Like that was going to do it.

Instead of a mild walk, I'd hurried back to the apartment, changed my clothes, and expected the gym to be empty like it was every other time I came down. I was pleasantly surprised to see Faith and even more so that she was willing to have a conversation. Most people crank up their tunes and don't even make eye contact during their workout. Exercising isn't a religious experience for me. It's a way to stay active and to keep away the fifteen extra pounds that keep threatening to find me.

My weight has always fluctuated up and down, much to the chagrin of my mother and the embarrassment of my sister. For years I'd starve myself, subsisting on chicken, fish, salads, and black coffee. One day I simply said enough. If I'm careful, work out regularly, and don't eat too many doughnuts, bowls of ice cream, or French fries, I can maintain my weight. I carry a few extra pounds, but I'm healthy and comfortable, and I don't care what anyone thinks. I could starve myself for a month before this annual vacation, but I refuse to. That's one of the joys of being a grown woman.

I thought about Faith as I walked down the corridor to my parents' apartment. The fifteenth deck was by far the most opulent in terms of apartments. Excluding the interiors, the lavish decorations and amenities lessened the closer to the waterline the decks were. I wondered where Faith and the other crewmembers lived. Was it dormitory style with ten or twelve to a room? Did each one have their own apartment, or at least a separate room? Did she have a roommate? If she did, that would make sharing her bunk as impossible as sharing my king-size bed in the A suite.

I had to stop thinking about things like bare skin and sleeping arrangements, or I'd never get any sleep tonight. Even though the apartment was well insulated, I'd left my vibrator at home, and I'd have to take care of business the old-fashioned way if it came to that.

My father was watching the news when I came out after a quick shower and even quicker climax.

"Have a good workout?" he asked, barely taking his eyes off the TV. Martin Chief was on the BBC anchor desk this evening. He was older than dirt and desperately needed to stop dying his hair. He was my father's favorite.

"Yes, thanks." That was all I said. I'd left a note on the counter, not that they'd worry. He didn't ask how many reps I did on what machine. I'm not sure he'd even know how to turn on the treadmill.

"That president of ours," he said, breaking the silence and pointing to our forty-fifth president. "He is exactly what this country needs. Someone who's not afraid to fire the first shot if it's warranted."

My father and I don't see eye to eye on politics, or much else for that matter. He is a staunch Republican and donates extensively to the Grand Old Party. I describe myself as a fiscal conservative and a social liberal. As a business owner who hopes to retire comfortably in twenty or so years, I am tight with my money and expect my elected officials to be the same. I believe in drug testing for welfare, Planned Parenthood, lower taxes, and smaller government. If I have to manage my business and personal finances according to a budget, the US government should be held to the same standards.

"What did he do now?" I asked, tired of trying to keep up with the obnoxious big mouth. Surprisingly, my father spent the next fifteen minutes giving me the blow-by-blow details of every tweet, email, press conference, and offhand comment our most senior elected official had produced that week.

I didn't agree with my father, but I was trying not to nod off. The hot shower and orgasm had definitely relaxed me. I jumped on an opening and said good night and left the room before he could engage me any further. My father doesn't say much, but then again, it's almost impossible to cut into any conversation around my mother, so when he gets a forum, he makes the most of it. I drank two glasses of water and crawled under the covers.

# Chapter Eight

*Day Two*
*At sea*
*Sydney to Hobart*

The sun was blistering bright where it came through the window. I'd forgotten to close the drapes when I came to bed and winced at the sharp pain that shot through my eyes. I was on my back, my knees up, my hand between my legs. I must have assumed this position along with one of the hottest dreams I'd had in a long, long time.

I rolled onto my side, pulling up the covers, as the air-conditioning was cooling my bare skin. If my mother had walked in during my dream, she probably would have fainted. It wouldn't have mattered that I was a grown woman and she'd walked in on me. I sleep naked at home but never when I'm traveling. I didn't remember taking off my jammies, but that too must've been a part of my dream. It was unsettling to think I might have actually made as much noise as I had in my head.

My back to the sun, I relaxed, my thoughts immediately returning to Faith. My goodness, she was young. I'm not normally attracted to women that much younger than me. They were usually flighty and clueless about anything other than themselves. However good in bed they were, the sex wasn't worth the vacancy in their eyes. I know not all young women are like that, but the ones I've come in contact with have been.

Faith had a mature worldliness about her that probably came from her travels, and that type of exposure gave you a different perspective on life. Granted, I doubted the tours from the *Escape* went to places like Calcutta or Haiti or other impoverished countries. She was interesting, and I enjoyed talking to her. I didn't have to find a topic or pretend I was interested in what she was saying. We weren't engaging in verbal foreplay or verbal sparring, but were simply two people having a stimulating conversation.

I glanced at the clock, surprised it was after nine. I'm normally up by six, including when I'm here. Nothing like a good dream about sex to knock you out. I got up, put on a robe, and made a cup of coffee, using the small Keurig on the table. Then I opened my laptop to check my email. When you own a business, you're never really away. You just work somewhere else.

Ninety minutes later, showered, dressed, and a full cup of coffee in hand, I was ready to undertake my daughterly duties. Today began with brunch on the patio catered by the bistro where I had met Faith the day before. I didn't believe in karma or kismet or mystical connections. We didn't need to engage a wedding planner and pick out a china pattern. The *Escape* simply offered a limited number of choices, and my parents always used The Cuppa for brunch.

I paid more attention to the conversation than I had during dinner and didn't have to suffer through another volley of Victoria's harsh sideways glances. However, my thoughts did keep drifting to Faith.

She was beautiful when her eyes lit up. She used her hands when she talked to make a point. She was engaging, amusing, optimistic, smart, sensitive, and just downright interesting. I couldn't remember anyone holding my attention or piquing my curiosity in a long time.

"Lowe, are you seeing anyone?" my mother asked, shocking the hell out of me. We never, and I mean never, discuss my social life.

"No one serious," I replied carefully. I wasn't sure where this question came from, and I was equally unsure if I wanted this topic to continue.

"I do hope you're looking for an appropriate life partner," my mother said, and I had to keep myself from falling off my chair.

Life partner? That label went out with the turn of the century.

"Meaning?" I asked, even though I suspected I knew her definition.

"Someone respectable," Victoria added helpfully. "From a good family. Someone who shares our interests, that will fit in. We wouldn't want them to feel uncomfortable around us." Translation: rich, white, and preferably male.

"I appreciate your concern about the woman who, someday, will want me to share the rest of her life," I said, clearly setting the expectation of any future wife I may or may not have.

"It's just that you're so busy with your job. How are you going to meet someone? Do you get out much?" my mother asked, calmly lifting her coffee cup to her perfectly applied lipstick mouth.

Get out much? What did that mean, and what in the hell was she fishing for? Victoria was most likely eager for my answer. However, in her designer vacation clothes and perfectly coiffed big hair, she looked only politely interested. I knew better. She was completely interested. Oh, and I hated the way my mother referred to my company, the company I built from the ground up with no help from them, as "my job." Like I worked on an assembly line.

"I am busy, but I do get out." Sometimes for the sole purpose of going back in, I thought, but didn't say for obvious reasons. Maybe someday I will. "I have a few good friends that I see on a regular basis." Friends with benefits was more accurate. "I meet people all the time."

"Why don't we ever meet them?" Victoria asked, sounding a bit snarky.

"Well," I said, "for starters, you live in Philadelphia, and our parents live here." I extended my arms toward the ocean. "None of you ever come to my house, and they can't come here." Nor would they want to, I thought, except one, and that was Charlotte. She'd come just to watch the fireworks.

"We just don't know much about what's going on in your life," Victoria said. "You are a member of the family."

"What do you want to know?" I probably should have asked, what do you want to know the answer to.

"You know, things," Victoria said, as if that was specific enough.

"Okay." I thought a minute. "I have season tickets to the Phoenix Symphony and an annual pass to the Phoenix Art Museum. This year I went to the Bolshoi ballet when it came to town, Cirque du Soleil, and the Broadway play *Hamilton*." My mother and sister showed their approval, but I knew they would soon rescind it.

"I also have season tickets to the Arizona Cardinals, Phoenix Mercury, and our new soccer team, the Phoenix Rising. I'm not much of a hockey fan, I'm afraid." As expected, their approving smiles diminished as I recited the names of our professional sports teams. "On the first Saturday of the month, I kayak with a bunch of women. Oh, and I have a library card," I added, just for the hell of it. My mother swallowed her distaste of my extracurricular activities.

"Do you sit on any boards?" Victoria asked.

"No. I prefer to contribute in a more meaningful way, with my checkbook." That was a not-so-subtle jab at her.

"When are you planning to quit?" my mother asked.

"Quit what?"

Victoria answered the question for her. "Your job."

That was a stupid question, and I almost told her so. "I own a business. You don't just quit. "I love what I do. Until I don't, I'll keep doing it."

"What are your expansion plans?" My father finally added to the conversation. I was thankful for the change in subject, but I looked at him carefully. He'd asked me that yesterday. Was he getting forgetful or just grabbing at something to say? I repeated my answer from the day before and added, "I'm at a comfortable size right now. I'll see how it plays out."

I reached for the other half of my bagel and saw my mother and Victoria exchange a knowing glance. To hell with them, I thought, taking a bite.

"We dock in Hobart tomorrow," my mother said. "Have you arranged to take any of the excursions? I'm told there is fabulous shopping."

"Maybe. I haven't decided," I fibbed. I'd been thumbing through the excursion book when I ran into Faith. Was it only yesterday?

"You're welcome to join Victoria and me."

My mother's view of shopping and mine are completely opposite. I'd rather have a tooth pulled with no anesthesia than go with them. I had thought about browsing the local outdoor market, where I could get a better idea and feel of the country than I could at a well-dressed, upscale mall.

"Like I said, I haven't decided. Don't wait for me." I wasn't sure, but I thought I saw a look of relief pass between them.

"I'm going to go hit some balls," my father said, getting up from the table.

"I'll walk with you." I grabbed the opportunity to get away from this conversation. "I need a little exercise to shake off this jet lag. Would either of you care to join me?" It was a rhetorical question. Neither of them would.

Our first day at sea after leaving Sydney I was assigned to work in one of the coffee shops in the morning, then moved to the patio bar.

The pool on the *Escape* was much smaller than the ones on a traditional cruise ship, but it did have the requisite lounge chairs and tables with umbrellas for shade from the harsh sun. The chairs were still in the same neat little rows the deck stewards put them in last night, like little toy soldiers waiting for their assignment. Several kids were playing in the water, their parents and grandparents watching nearby. Mr. Locklear from deck eight approached.

"Hi, Faith. Can I get three diets and a glass of ice water?" Karl Locklear was a large, rotund man with jet-black hair dyed for too many years. He had to be in his seventies, yet he didn't have one gray hair on his head. His bare chest, on the other hand, looked like a pad of steel wool had exploded on it.

I filled the large plastic cups with ice as he pointed out who was who in and around the pool. But I lost track of what he was saying when Lowe strolled into the area and grabbed a towel from the stack from the table by the Jacuzzi. I didn't hear a word after she dropped her towel on the chair and shucked her shirt. I almost dropped the cup when she stepped out of her shorts. Mr. Locklear was still talking, and I just wanted him to go away so I could ogle Lowe in private.

Lowe was wearing a one-piece suit that accentuated every womanly part on her body. When she dove into the pool with barely a ripple, I knew she spent a lot of time in the water. I waited eagerly for her to resurface, and when she did, my heart started beating again.

Luckily, other than the Locklear family, no one else was in the area, and I had an unobstructed view of Lowe as she swam lap after short lap. Her strong arms cut through the water, and I felt like a voyeur just standing there watching her. We'd met little more than twenty-four hours ago, but I was completely enthralled.

One of the Locklear grandkids interrupted my leering and asked for another glass of water. I filled up his cup and quickly shooed him off to continue my new favorite pastime.

Lowe swam nonstop for at least twenty minutes before effortlessly lifting herself out of the pool. Water slid off her body, leaving a trail to the chair. She toweled off her hair, then her arms and legs, before lying down and stretching out.

From my vantage point, I watched the rapid rise and fall of her perfect breasts as she cooled down from her workout.

Not long after, other residents joined the Locklears, and I had to do my job instead of stare at Lowe. I had my back to the pool replacing a bottle of gin when I heard a voice that make a tickle skip down my spine.

"May I have a refill?"

Lowe stood behind me as I took a deep breath before turning around. Instead of forty feet away, she was four, and I could see a hint of an old tan line on her shoulder.

"Sure."

Lowe handed me her thermal mug. "Water, please."

"Enjoy your swim?" I asked, then immediately regretted my question. It let her know I was aware of what she'd been doing.

"Yes, I did. Thanks. I've been so busy getting ready for this trip I haven't been to the gym in a couple of weeks."

"Do you swim regularly?" I handed her back her mug, reminding myself not to look at her exceptional cleavage.

"I have a pool in my backyard, and I try to get in it every day."

"How long have you been swimming," I asked out of politeness to a guest of a resident. Yeah, right. However much I wanted to watch her walk away, I wanted her to stay more.

"Five or six years."

"Enjoying your trip so far?" God, Faith, that was stupid. We were barely eighteen hours out of port.

Lowe looked at me for a long time, and when her hot eyes traced down my body and back up again, I forgot what I'd asked.

"I'm definitely enjoying myself, thank you."

Another resident needed my attention at the other end of the bar, so I excused myself. I was only able to catch a glimpse of Lowe's backside as she walked back to the chair. I was so distracted, I overfilled the man's glass and had to start over. When Lowe gathered up her towel and bag and left, I was disappointed yet grateful to be able to focus on my job.

I somehow managed to get through the rest of my shift and back to my cabin without seeing her again.

## CHAPTER NINE

I could see lights off the starboard bow and knew we'd be docking in the morning. I'd signed up to be a concierge for one of the tours and couldn't wait to get off the ship. I'd been feeling edgy the last few days, which meant I needed a change of scenery. I needed to feel solid ground beneath my feet and smell clean, salt-free air. Normally we had to shell out cash if we were going on one of the tours, but because I agreed to work, the *Escape* paid my expenses. I looked at my watch. I had eight minutes to get to the auditorium where the briefing was being held. Like I said earlier, the *Escape* brought in local experts to provide residents with information about the country we were about to visit. We weren't required to attend, but I wanted to be as prepared as I could be.

The room was crowded, and an African-American man in white pants and a red button-down shirt under a blue blazer stood in front of the room. He adjusted the microphone on his lapel.

After the requisite "Check, check, check, can you hear me?" the man greeted us. "Good evening, ladies and gentlemen." The crowd settled down, the noisy chatter dissipating. I grabbed an empty seat in the last row.

As he talked I took a few notes on the brochures I'd picked up from the table in the lobby. The man explained the various packages and timelines. There were several to choose from, ranging from those that were wheelchair accessible to those more strenuous. Busses would depart from the dock at eight and drop passengers off at an exclusive mall, the beach, hiking trails, the farmers' market, and a few other places. They would make a return run in the opposite direction later that evening. If residents missed the appointed time, they were on their own, the man warned them several times. He, of course, was much more eloquent, but the message was the same.

I was reading the map on the island when someone sat down beside me.

"Do you come here often?"

I laughed at the lame pick-up line. "You're not serious?" I asked Lowe.

"Absolutely. Does the *Escape* stop here often?" she asked, trying hard to look innocent.

"We've been here before. You?"

"First time."

Something about those two words made me think about how it would be our first time together. I had to get that image out of my head.

"Hey," Lowe said, snapping her fingers. "Since you've been here and I haven't, why don't you show me around?"

And I must have looked like I was going to say no because she quickly said, "It's more fun that way. And if we get lost, two heads can think better than one. Besides, I suck at map reading."

Lowe looked so innocent and devilishly handsome, she almost took my breath away.

"I imagine you can find your way around anything." My voice was more seductive than teasing, and Lowe obviously picked up on the difference. "I don't think we'd be interested in the same things," I added quickly.

Lowe's eyes darkened, and she was looking at my lips when she said, "I kind of hoped we could be." This time her voice was soft and whispery.

"Ms. Carter," I said, dragging my eyes from hers and my mind out from between the sheets.

"I thought I asked you to call me Lowe."

"All right, Lowe."

"Let's just take the same tour and go to the same places at the same time," she said quickly. "I'm going on the B tour. We start at the Airwalk, then do some hang-gliding, a little shopping at Salamanca Place, and finish up with dinner at Franklin's. What are your plans?" she asked, looking at my notes.

I caught the scent of her cologne. It wasn't perfume but had a more textured scent, if I could explain it that way. She smelled good. My nipples instinctively hardened due to the proximity of her mouth to my breasts. I prayed she wouldn't notice, but how could she not?

"I knew it," she said triumphantly, pointing to the activities circled on my sheet. "We are going to the same places." She was almost beaming.

"Lowe." I started to explain I wasn't going to be a tourist. Every activity had a crew member along to take care of things. The residents paid a hefty fee every month to have just about anything they wanted at any time.

"Consider this part of your exceptional customer service."

My anger started to simmer. "I'm not an amenity," I said forcefully. This wasn't the first or the fourth or even the fourteenth time someone thought I came with the apartment purchase agreement. I was disappointed that Lowe had.

"What?" Lowe asked, her expression questioning. "No," she said quickly, catching my meaning. "God, no, no, no. That's not what I mean."

I looked at her long and hard, my bullshit meter on full alert.

"God, no, Faith. I apologize if that came out wrong. In no way, and I do mean absolutely no way, did I mean to imply or even think you would do that." She sat back in her seat and sighed heavily. "God, I've really fucked things up, haven't I?" she said more to herself than to me.

"No, you haven't," I said, making a decision I hoped I wouldn't regret. I changed the subject. "I overheard your name in the conversation among the staff today," I said carefully.

"This might not be good," Lowe said, not looking at me.

"They said you were nice." Lowe turned and looked at me.

"Nice?"

"Yes, nice. I'll be on the bus at eight."

# CHAPTER TEN

*Day Three*
*Hobart*

I tried not to look too obvious that I was anxious for breakfast to be over. Victoria and our mother were dressed for a day of shopping, and I would be spending the day with Faith. I hadn't slept much last night, anticipating if she would show up this morning. Finally, at 7:42, I was able to escape, so I left the apartment and ran down the hall to the stairs.

The line for my bus wasn't too long, and I made small talk with an Italian couple in front of me. They were visiting residents on deck eight and had also boarded in Sydney. When it was their turn at the sign-in desk, a familiar voice greeted them. I peeked over their shoulder and was surprised to see Faith sitting behind the table. It took me a moment to figure out that she was probably working the table, and after everyone was signed in, she'd be done.

When it was my turn, I said, "I didn't expect to see you here." The table Faith sat behind contained a stack of brochures of the activities and a basket of small tubes of sunscreen.

"I'm working the tour," she said, handing me a clipboard.

"Excuse me?" The two and two I'd just put together suddenly no longer added up to four.

"The tour. Every excursion organized by the *Escape* requires a crew member."

"And you're the crew member?" My anticipation of spending the day with her started to deflate. Yeah, I'd be with her all day, along with dozens of other people.

Faith nodded.

"What do you have to do?"

"I'm just on the scene in case any of the residents need anything. It's like a mini concierge," she explained.

"So, that's why you said you'd be on the bus this morning?"

The twinkle of teasing in Faith's eye didn't let me stay upset. "I did say I'd be on the bus at eight."

"Is that the only reason?" How could I have missed the signals I'd thought I was receiving? I tamped down my disappointment.

"What other reason would there be?"

I opened my mouth and started to tell her what I thought but changed my mind. I felt bad enough without adding public humiliation to my situation. "None, whatsoever," I said. "I guess I'll see you on the bus then." I signed the empty space next to my name and stepped to my left as Faith greeted the next passenger in line.

The ramp from the main deck to the dock had a gradual slope, and I was still shaking my head in disbelief when I stepped onto the dock. Three busses were lined up at the curb, each with a large black letter on a white background taped to the inside window of the first row.

I joined the growing crowd milling around by the door of the bus with the large B. I'd met a few of the residents on my previous visits, and we exchanged small talk as we waited for the driver and the person I now knew was our concierge.

"When did a concierge start accompanying the tours?" I asked the downstairs neighbor of my parents. We'd met on my last trip and had visited over cocktails and dinner several times.

"About eight months ago," the man said, glancing at his wife for verification. He then looked around like he didn't want anyone to hear what he was about to say. He stepped closer and lowered his voice. "I heard there was a problem with the authorities in one of the small, obscure countries we visited, and it created quite a ruckus. The grandson of one of the residents on a lower deck ended up in jail, and it took several days to get him out. I guess he raised holy hell and demanded the American Embassy be called." The man shook his head in clear disapproval. "I don't know what they had to do to get that boy out, but his grandparents moved out shortly after that. Rumor has it they had to sell their apartment to pay for his release." The man's wife nodded. "After that, someone from the ship is on every tour."

"Glorified babysitter, if you ask me," the wife added.

"What do they do?"

"Not much, at least on the tours we've been on. They just tag along and keep an eye on things, I guess," the man surmised.

"Except for Faith. She's wonderful," the woman said.

Naturally my ears perked up at the mention of Faith's name. "How so?"

"She's so nice," the woman said. "She's friendly, tells us a little bit about where we're going before we get there, and reminds us when to be back on the bus. She stays with us and answers questions and keeps us from getting lost."

"Or in trouble," the man said quickly.

"Ronald, we're all too old to get into trouble," his wife said, teasing him.

"She even helped me carry one of my bags back to the bus," the woman said, smiling and nodding as if it were the nicest thing anyone had ever done for her. "Faith is just so pleasant every time I see her. I was so glad to see she was on this tour."

"I don't think we've met." A tall woman with short gray hair and aviator sunglasses directed her comment to me as she approached our group.

"No, we haven't. I'm Lowe Carter." I held out my hand.

The woman shook it and placed her left hand on top of mine in a strong, two-handed grasp. "You're Francis and Landon's daughter," she said.

"Yes, ma'am. I am."

"Francis has told us about you. My name is Shirley Phillips. Are you the older or the younger one? I don't remember," Shirley asked, releasing my hand.

"My sister doesn't think so, but I am the oldest."

Shirley chuckled. "One of those sisters. I have two of them. How long are you visiting?"

"I'll be leaving when we return to Sydney."

"Well, welcome aboard. "She looked behind me. "Oh, here comes Faith."

"Everybody ready?" Faith asked, joining the crowd.

Murmurs of yeses spilled out from the passengers, and the couple's face lit up with excitement. I had to admit mine probably did as well. Faith wore a pair of low-cut, well-worn jeans, boots, a polo shirt adorned with the *Escape* logo, and a pale-green bandanna tied around her neck. A pair of sunglasses sat on the brim of her white cap, slightly obscuring the Nike logo. She had a blue bag slung over her shoulder. She looked ready to explore, and I was more than ready to explore her. I told my libido to settle down.

"I am so looking forward to this," she said, waving at the driver to open the door. "I need to feel my feet on solid ground for a while. Let's get going."

We started boarding the bus, and Faith greeted each passenger as she checked all the ID badges blowing in the strong morning breeze. She didn't treat me any different from the others as I climbed aboard the big blue bus.

"Is this seat taken?"

I looked up and into Faith's dark, amused eyes. I couldn't help but laugh at the tired pick-up line. I moved my backpack, and Faith set hers on the seat beside me.

"I thought you'd have to sit up front?"

Faith looked at me, a question on her face.

"One of the other passengers said you give an overview of where we're going."

"I do, but I stand in the front when I do. That doesn't mean I have to sit there as well."

"Again, my lucky day," I said, meaning it as the bus pulled away from the curb.

"I've got to get us started."

She stowed her bag in the seat beside me and walked the few rows to the front, where she picked up the microphone.

"Good morning, ladies and gentlemen," Faith greeted us, her voice clear and strong coming over the PA-system speakers. Several voices returned the greeting.

"I'd like to officially welcome you to Hobart. My name is Faith Williams, and I'm your concierge today. We're headed to the famous Tahune Airwalk, but before we leave, I'd like to give you a brief history of the island state of Hobart."

I watched Faith as she provided an overview of the state, its population, weather, and basic geographical information, including the fact that it was founded in 1804 as a penal colony.

"We'll be in Hobart until eleven pm tomorrow night, so you may want to take advantage of a drive up to Mount Wellington, visit the Royal Hobart Botanical Gardens, or even fly by helicopter to the Frogmore Creek Winery. We'll have plenty of time later this afternoon to stroll the waterfront cafés, restaurants, and art studios that overlook the harbor."

Faith talked for a few more minutes, then walked down the aisle answering questions and making small talk with the other passengers before returning to her seat beside me.

We rode in silence for about ten minutes, and I had to say something to get my mind off the feel of Faith's right hip, shoulder, arm, and leg pressed against mine in the narrow seats. The parts of my body in direct contact with Faith's were hot, the nerves sending all kinds of powerful messages to other parts of my body that would love to be against hers. Out of the corner of my eye, I could see the rise and fall of her breasts when she breathed, and I stole a glance more than a few times.

"What's the longest?"

"I beg your pardon?" Faith asked.

"You said you were ready to have your feet on solid ground. What's the longest you've been at sea?"

"Oh, right. Seventeen days."

"Wow. Don't you get like scurvy or something like that?"

Faith laughed and finally looked at me.

"No, we don't get scurvy. That was back in the Christopher Columbus days. I just miss the smell of dirt and trees. Don't get me wrong, I love what I do, but a change of pace is good once in a while."

"Did you always want to be on a ship and sail around the world?"

"When I was young I couldn't wait to get out of my village and into the big city."

I detected a note of nostalgia in her voice.

"And now you're on a floating city. Do you get any time off when you dock?" I asked, wanting to know how she spent her spare time.

"Most of the time. They try to work the schedule so that everyone can have at least one day on shore. I don't mind this," she said, waving around her. "It's the best of both worlds. I get to experience the activities just like everyone else does."

"But you have to keep one eye on us? In case we wander off or get in trouble," I added to see if she'd bite at the rumor the man had told me about earlier. She didn't.

"Not really. I'm just here if anyone needs anything they can't get themselves."

"Have you ever had to intervene before something got messy?"

Faith laughed again, and my insides did a little flip-flop.

"No, not hardly. Although one time I had to find some tomato juice when one of the passengers got too close to a skunk. That was the longest ride back to the ship I've ever had. We had to open all the windows, or we never would have made it back."

Now that we were talking, I could look at Faith without being impolite. She was so young, her face smooth with only the hint of a laugh line around her eyes. Her profile was strong, and I loved hearing her accent when she spoke. I liked saying her name. It was feminine, just like her.

I don't normally fall for femmes. Actually, they kind of scare me sometimes. I normally go for women that take less time to get ready than I do. Not hard-core butch, but somewhere in the middle.

Faith, on the other hand, was further to the left of butch than I'd ever been.

"Are the crew like sailors on shore leave?" I was again rewarded with the low timbre of Faith's laugh. God, I could listen to that for the rest of my life.

"Some of them. Others have family back home and behave."

"What about you?"

Faith turned in her seat a little to look at me. Her leg pressed harder against mine, but then she pulled away.

"I don't act like a sailor, but I do get off every chance I get."

Heat shot through me, and I tried not to squirm in my seat. The temperature in the bus shot up at least ten degrees.

"Well, uh," I barely managed to get out, not having a clue what to say to that.

"Oh my god, that's not what I meant." She buried her face in her hands. "Why do I keep saying stupid things when I'm around you?" Her voice was muffled.

I leaned close to her, my lips almost brushing her ear, and said quietly, "Because you're captivated by my ravishingly good looks, riveted by my charming personality, and..." I hesitated until she drew back and looked at me warily through her fingers. "Because I'm nice." I could have said something like "because you know I want you," but I settled for the descriptor she'd used yesterday. She dropped her hands, the tension between us lessening.

"Yeah, right. That's it," she said, her eyes sparkling. "Does your sister go with you?"

"What?" I asked, completely confused because all the blood in my brain had settled in my crotch.

"Your sister," Faith repeated. "Does she come with you on any of the excursions?"

I finally figured out she had completely changed the subject. Smart girl. "No. She and my mother enjoy more sedate sightseeing. They're on the shopping-mall bus." I indicated it with my thumb over my shoulder.

"I don't remember seeing your parents' names on many of the other tours we've done."

"I'm not surprised," I answered. My core temperature was lower than it had been a few moments ago, but still not back to normal. It probably wouldn't be until I got off this bus. "I don't know what they do all day every day. My dad plays golf every chance he gets, but even that can get old, I suppose." I had never understood the allure of golf. I'd rather compete against someone.

"He does sign up for the golf tours." Faith corrected herself. "I see your mother in the lounge talking or having lunch with the other residents. Occasionally I'll spot her on the top deck. But it's none of my business, and I shouldn't be reporting their activities to you. Our residents value their privacy."

Valuable privacy was more like it. For what they paid for their unit, my parents should be able to commit murder and expect no one to say anything. Just then the driver slammed on his brakes. A few passengers shrieked.

"You okay?" I asked Faith as we came to a stop. My stomach was somewhere in the middle of my throat.

"Yes," she said, getting out of her seat. "Is everyone all right?"

Murmurs of "yes" and "I think so" came from around me as Faith moved up and down the aisle checking on everyone.

Traffic was terrible, and we were stuck in the middle of it. Faith returned after conferring with the driver and saying a few calming words to the passengers.

"This is nothing like my morning commute," I said sarcastically.

"I can't complain about mine," Faith said. "I don't know how people do it."

"I know. I'm lucky. I work primarily from home, but when I have to go into a store, I can pretty much pick a time."

"Even luckier."

"Do you plan on making the *Escape* your career?"

"God, no," she said quickly, then blushed like she'd said something she shouldn't have. "Don't get me wrong," she said. "I love my job, but it's hard work and not practical if you want to have a family."

"Do you?" I asked, curious. Normally I never asked the question because I didn't want to know the answer. I certainly never wanted to open up that line of conversation with a date. I'd concluded that I wasn't the settling-down type. My job was demanding, and I grew bored easily, at least when it came to women. Not many had held my attention longer than a few weeks. Even fewer for longer than a few months. I loved my job and my life, which included coming and going when I wanted and with whom I wanted.

"Yes, I do," Faith said firmly.

"Any prospects?" Another question I didn't think I wanted to know the answer to. I could plead ignorance when it came to my pursuit of her.

"This life isn't the best way to have a relationship. And it certainly isn't the ideal way to find one either," Faith replied, not answering my question.

"No shipboard romances?"

"No."

"Do you—"

"I'm sorry. It's time for me to go to work," Faith said abruptly.

If I wasn't mistaken, Faith had used her job as an excuse to end our conversation. It really was none of my business if or who she dated, but I was curious about the type of woman Faith would be interested in. I'd almost asked if she'd be interested in getting together, aka have sex, but she must have sensed the direction I was headed. I'd have to plan my next approach more carefully.

## CHAPTER ELEVEN

I'd begun to think a lot about the next few years and what I was going to do after my time on the *Escape*. I loved my job, but I wanted a normal life with a wife, my own house, and maybe even a dog. I know that sounds like motherhood and apple pie, but it is what it is. I certainly wasn't going to tell a rich, successful, sophisticated woman like Lowe that I wanted to be a wife and a mother. But until my life's landscape changed, I had work to do. Lowe's questions were starting to make me uncomfortable, and I took a convenient way out. I reached for the microphone.

"Ladies and gentlemen, may I have your attention." A few people stopped talking, and I repeated my introduction. "We're at the Tahune Airwalk."

Everyone stared at me, silent, and I sensed their anticipation and excitement pick up, Lowe's included. I continued. "The Airwalk gives a stunning view of Hobart's southern forests. You'll find a treetop walkway that is forty-five meters from the ground, and the Swinging Bridges Track has two steel-cable footbridges that cross the rivers. Several other paths are clearly marked, where you can sit and enjoy the clean, fresh scent of the forest, birdwatch, or just relax. For those who are more adventurous, you'll find hang gliding and a new zip line." Several of the passengers gave a chorus of whoops.

"The bus will be here for three hours, so take your time and enjoy the beautiful countryside."

The driver hit a switch, and the door opened with a loud hiss. I was the first one off, followed by the driver and the passengers. Lowe stepped off somewhere in the middle of the mix of residents and guests.

Lowe and I, along with Shirley and five others from the bus, joined a young couple at the briefing area to the zip-line course. After endless paperwork we were taken to a small patio area and given a fifteen-minute safety briefing. We were fitted with what our guide, Kendrick, called a sit harness that would secure us to the line. The harness buckled at the waist, and the thick, reinforced nylon wrapped around each thigh was adjusted snugly with a series of buckles and straps. My helmet was bright yellow and smelled like disinfectant. Twelve minutes later, all safe and secure, we tracked single file to the first platform. The newlyweds were first, Lowe and I bringing up the rear.

Conversation on the trail was peppered with excited, nervous chatter. The newlyweds were debating who would go first, and the couple directly in front of Lowe and me were having an argument, their voices tense through gritted teeth. The bride's new ring sparkled in the sunlight, and I thought she was crazy for wearing it out here where it could get lost. Then again, if I had two carats glittering on my finger, I'd probably never take it off either.

The trail veered to the left, and we began a steep climb upward, making conversation difficult. I didn't know if it was out of politeness or something else, but somehow, I always found myself climbing the trail in front of Lowe. I knew her eyes were on me, and it wasn't to make sure she didn't run into me.

The trees around us were thick and at times created a canopy over our heads, in other places thinning out and allowing the midday sun to warm our skin.

Large rocks made rough steps, providing much-needed traction on the steep incline. The group spread out, as some were in better shape than others. The man of the arguing couple in front of us complained the entire time. Lowe was breathing easily and had adjusted her pace to match my slower one. Among the distinct disadvantages of being short, this was one of them.

At the first platform, Kendrick reiterated the safety features and instructions on how to step off the deck, steer, and approach the platform on the other side. A few people asked questions, and the new husband stepped up first, showing his bride how brave he was. He shuffled to the edge and stopped, a look of complete terror replacing the bravado that had been on his face the entire climb. His wife cheered him on, but he didn't move. His legs were shaking, and in a weak, girly voice, he said he couldn't do it. Kendrick stood beside him and spoke about the safety features of the line and how everything was made in Australia. I guess that information was supposed to make him feel better.

The groom shook his head and said, "Somebody's going to have to push me." A split second later his wife did. He screamed all the way across the line while the rest of us cheered.

"That's the way to show him who's boss, honey. Start him out right," Shirley said, joking. The wife went next.

"I'd love to be a fly on her helmet when she gets to the other side," Lowe said.

I'd been on zip lines before in Hawaii and Brazil, but every line was a new adventure. The scenery today was spectacular, and I wasn't just talking about Lowe, who stood close beside me. She was wearing a pair of loose-fit Levis, which looked great on her. Her boots were well worn, and her belt was some canvas thing with a utility buckle. Her light-blue shirt had matching breast pockets just below a Columbia tag. Her long sleeves were rolled up messily above her elbows, showing off her tan arms. She looked like she was comfortable outdoors. A large black watch with several dials and buttons was buckled around her right wrist. I'd noticed that she was left-handed and had always found something really sexy about a lefty.

"I suppose one zip line is like another," she said, referring to my earlier comment about how many different ones I'd been on.

"Actually, no. The mechanics are the same, but every one I've seen is different. Every time on a new line is like the first time."

Lowe arched her eyebrows, and I realized she'd taken my comment suggestively. Either I had better start thinking before opening my mouth, or she'd better get laid soon and get me off her radar. That thought wasn't a pleasant one. I stepped onto the platform.

Kendrick, who looked no older than seventeen, gave me the same briefing as he had provided the eight people before me. I had to pay attention to understand him through his thick local accent. Because I had no questions, he promptly secured my pulley to the line with a bright-red locking carabiner and attached the safety line directly behind that. He checked my harness, ensuring everything that would hold me from falling into the trees below was ready to go and in the right position. He then slid the straps around my thighs up to just below my butt and secured them snugly. Finally, he checked with his crewmate on the other end of the one-hundred-meter line before giving me a thumbs-up. I knew Lowe was watching me, and I grabbed the steering handle above my head and took a running leap off the deck.

The weight of my body hit the harness, digging the three-inch nylon into the back of my thighs. It wasn't painful, just uncomfortable, and I quickly forgot about it as I sailed through the air. The sun was at my back, the cool breeze blowing across my face. It was quiet, the only sound the pulley gliding across the metal line. The trees were thick and green, and I couldn't see the ground through the thick foliage. It smelled wet and fresh.

I started to rotate to the right, so I adjusted the steering handle to correct the movement as the landing platform rapidly approached. I relaxed and raised my legs as I got closer. The braking system abruptly slowed me down, jerking me forward. My face hit the pulley and I saw stars for a moment. I wasn't hurt, but the blow was completely unexpected. Ten feet from the platform, I slowed even further, and my feet hit the hard wood softly. Six steps more and I was safely aboard.

Martin, our other guide, unbuckled me and asked if I had any questions. Then he made a few suggestions on my technique before reaching for his radio. I stepped off the platform onto the dirt as he told Kendrick to send the next person over.

The couple was still arguing, and the newlyweds were kissing as I maneuvered where I could watch Lowe sail across the treetops. She'd never been on a zip line, and the expression on her face as she approached the platform showed her joy.

"That was awesome," she said as she stepped toward me after Martin unhooked her.

Her face flushed and her eyes glowing, she was radiant and beautiful. My stomach dropped a little, and I reminded myself nothing could come of this.

I don't remember what we talked about as we traversed the next three platforms, too caught up in Lowe beside me. My senses were on high alert, every nerve taking everything in. I must have made coherent conversation because Lowe never asked me to repeat anything or looked at me strangely.

As we approached the fourth line, we stopped and had a light snack courtesy of the zip-line company. A box of assorted granola and power bars sat next to a bright-orange Igloo cooler with white paper cups stacked neatly on the lid. Everyone in our group took turns reaching into the box, and when it was Lowe's turn, she held up the selections in my direction. I snagged a chocolate-chip power bar because it was easier to pretend that the thick, chewy texture was a yummy candy bar.

Sweets are my weakness, my downfall, and my Achilles heel. I'll pass up any other food to have a doughnut, a cookie, or a bag of M&Ms. I'll finish the last doughnut in the box the morning after they're brought in, all of which is another reason I always work out at the gym. I don't know if I go to the gym because I eat so much crap or I eat crap as a reward for going to the gym. Either way it doesn't matter, because I've managed to maintain my size with minimal effort.

Lowe handed me a cup of water, our fingers touching as I reached for it. Our eyes locked. Judging by the look in hers, I knew the same thing was going on inside her as was going on inside me. A bolt of desire shot up my arm, whizzed through my chest, and landed right where I knew it would. My face flushed, and I came alive all over. Lowe must have seen my reaction because her eyes widened, recognition and desire reflected at me.

This is ridiculous, I thought. We're in the middle of a hot, humid jungle, surrounded by other people. I had an unflattering harness wrapped around me like a pretzel and a bright-yellow cooking pot on my head. It had been quite a workout, climbing the trail up to this spot, and I'm sure I had sweat and dirt all over my face. But the expression on Lowe's face told me that none of that mattered.

"Thanks," I said, finding my voice and taking the cup from her.

"My goodness, this is quite an adventure," Shirley said, breaking through my lustful haze. She sat on the bench to my left.

"Yes, it is," I replied after a moment, grateful for the interruption. "How are you doing?"

"Well, these old bones aren't what they used to be, but I'm not dead yet," she replied, making fun of herself. Lowe sat down beside me.

We chatted for a few more minutes until break time was over and the first person stepped onto the next platform.

The last line was, by far, the longest, at over seven hundred feet. I stepped up first, more to get away from the bickering couple, and jumped. I let go of the steering handle and stretched out my arm and legs like I was skydiving. I arched my back, almost flipping over, my back parallel to the ground. The sky was crystal clear, and in this position, all I heard was the rush of the wind in my ears. Far too soon, I righted myself and prepared to land.

After the last person hit the deck, we hiked back to the main staging area. Kendrick was pointing out native vegetation while Martin told god-awful jokes, and I stumbled over an exposed tree root. Lowe grabbed me around the waist, and I fell against her. Her body was hard yet soft in all the right places, and she smelled like a mixture of sweat, outdoors, exercise, and woman. Being so close to her almost made me stumble again. We stopped, the others continuing up the trail.

"You okay?" she asked, her arms still around me.

The top of my head just met her chin, and I had to look up to peer into her eyes. What I saw almost made my heart stop. In an instant her blue eyes turned dark, transforming from concern to desire. Her arms around me tightened, and my heart raced, my mouth suddenly very dry. Her eyes shifted to my lips, tracing their outline. I'd seen that look before, the one right before I was going to be kissed by someone who knew how. Lowe bent her head toward me.

I needed to stop this. This was not a good idea, and nothing was going to come of it. At least nothing other than sheer pleasure, if my instincts were right. And they were never, ever wrong. I settled against her, wanting nothing else in the world at this exact moment except to feel Lowe's lips on mine. I reached up, my hand on the back of her neck.

"Hey, you two."

I jumped away from Lowe like we'd just been caught by her father in the basement with the lights off.

"Everything all right?" Kendrick asked, rounding the corner.

"Yeah, sure," Lowe replied. "Sorry we fell behind."

Kendrick looked from me to Lowe, then back at me. He knew exactly what we'd been doing. Or, to be precise, almost done. One more second and he would have gotten an eyeful. The way he smiled at us told me he'd probably seen more.

Lowe held out her hand toward me, her eyes still burning. "Come on. We need to catch up."

I looked at her hand and was finally in control enough to use my brain instead of my crotch to guide me. I ignored it and started walking toward the rest of the group.

Back at the gear shack, Lowe stepped forward and reached for the buckle on my harness.

"Let me help you with that."

I stepped back quickly, needing distance between us. If Lowe helped me, I couldn't possibly get out of this harness without her touching me. I didn't need that kind of temptation now.

Lowe looked at me, surprise clear on her face.

"Thanks," I said quickly, keeping my tone light. "I can get it." I put my helmet on the shelf and ran my fingers through my hair several times, rubbing my scalp. I'm sure I had helmet hair, like all the other women, except for Lowe, whose hair was so short, it didn't matter. I'd often toyed with the idea of cutting mine. It fell below my shoulders and was thick and hard to maintain, especially in humid climates. I don't think I'd have the nerve to cut it as short as Lowe's, but if I did, it would give me more much-needed sleep time.

My hands were shaking so hard I could barely open the buckle at my waist, and I turned to the side so my distress wasn't so obvious. After I finally got it unfastened, the weight of the heavy material slid the harness down my legs, and it landed with a thump at my feet. I stepped out of it, picked it up, and hung it alongside several others on a bright-red hook on the wall.

"Ladies and gentlemen, we invite you to step inside the office. Check out our souvenirs or any other items you find you just can't live without," Kendrick said, pointing to the office where we'd signed our paperwork. I'd noticed racks of long-sleeved T-shirts in one corner and several shelves on the wall with hats and cups, all displaying the Airwalk Adventures logo.

I'd just sent money to my mum and didn't have much to spare, so I sat on a bright-yellow bench beside the door when everyone but Lowe went inside. She sat down beside me, her leg touching mine. We had plenty of room on the bench, but she obviously wasn't going to let me get away from the closeness of our almost-kiss on the trail.

"No shopping?"

"No, not today."

"With as many years you've been on the *Escape* and the places you've been, I bet you have souvenirs from dozens of countries."

"Not as many as you'd think," I said. "My cabin's pretty small."

"I've always wondered where the crew lived. Do you have your own cabin, apartment, room, bunk?" She rattled off the various choices of living arrangements.

"All of the above, but I do have my own. The captain and the senior crew have their own apartments, obviously not nearly as luxurious as the residents'. Some have small cabins they share, and, therefore, some have a bunk."

"What about Faith? Do you share?"

I looked at Lowe again. The way her lips moved mesmerized me. My skin heated just thinking about them traveling over me, demanding that I respond. Like that would be a hardship. I was already halfway there. Lowe Carter could be trouble, and I needed to go very far and very fast from this woman.

Lowe's eyes shifted from my lips and bored into mine. Fire and desire burned in her dark pupils, and my mouth went dry.

"No, I don't," I said seriously.

Lowe quirked an eyebrow and nodded. "Neither do I."

I couldn't stop my heart from racing. The idea of being Lowe's one and only short-circuited my mind. That she would, as the wedding vow goes, forsake all others for me made me limp. It was a heady thought to be the sole focus of her attention.

## Chapter Twelve

The bus ride down the hill was more subdued than the ride up, everyone tired from the fresh air and exercise. I think I even heard someone snoring in one of the seats behind us.

"That was fun," I said, breaking the tense silence between us. When Faith had boarded, I saw her glancing around the bus, probably looking for a place to sit other than next to me. She obviously hadn't found one because she was beside me, yet keeping her distance.

"I'm glad you liked it," she replied professionally.

"Shirley is quite a character."

"Yes, she is. Her husband passed away several years ago, and now she spends all her time on the *Escape*."

"How old is she?" I asked, anything to keep the conversation moving.

"I'm not sure. Probably in her mid-sixties. Her children are in their forties, I think."

"Do they visit her frequently?" I'd often wondered if other residents saw their kids once a year like my parents did.

"All the time," Faith said, loosening up a bit. "They come at least every other month, I think. It's hard to keep track sometimes."

"What did she and her husband do?" What I really wanted to know was where they got the money to live on the *Escape*. My parents never said how much they paid for their apartment, but when they were first considering buying I'd done some research and gasped at the prices.

"I'm not sure." Faith scrunched her lips. "I think he was in banking or something like that."

"So that's where all the interest I pay goes. Must have been quite a bank," I said sarcastically. That remark finally brought a smile to Faith's lips. And my god, what lips they were.

My heart raced at the memory of almost kissing her back on the trail. If Kendrick hadn't come looking for us I would have, no doubt about it. The way Faith had been looking at me and when she licked her lips, I'm sure she would have kissed me back. The feel of her hand on my neck and the slight pressure pulling me toward her was showstopping. After watching her backside as she climbed the trail and the way her harness accentuated her breasts and hips, who knows what would have happened after that. I felt ridiculously like a teenager.

I've dated a lot of women for a lot of years, and it had been a long, long time since I'd experienced the level of anticipation I felt with Faith. Her bare leg was inches from mine, and I wanted to touch it, feel her warmth, run my fingers up and down her skin. I wanted to feel her muscles react, quiver with desire and spasm in release. My right leg started to bounce up and down, something I do when I'm nervous. Faith looked at it, and I forced myself to stop.

She had to know I was attracted to her. All the signals were there, the spark between us crackling. What was the point of denying it? Why fight it? We were two grown women. If we wanted the same thing, a pleasant way to pass the time, then why not? I'd always been the rational one, the one who looked at all sides thoughtfully and logically. Emotions rarely came into play because facts and common sense were much more reliable. I had three weeks, no, make that twenty days until I left the *Escape* and went back to Phoenix. Why waste time?

"Faith," I said, but she cut me off.

"No." Her voice was barely above a whisper.

"You don't even know what I was going to say." She looked at me like I was crazy. "Okay, you know what I was going to say," I admitted, keeping my own voice down. The people around us didn't need to hear our conversation or listen to me beg. "You didn't even give me a chance."

"The answer would still be the same."

"But you didn't hear me out." God, I sounded desperate. But then again, wasn't I?

"No need for you to waste your time."

"But—"

"But no. It's not going to happen."

An image of "it" flashed through my mind, and I couldn't give up. I was not a quitter. "May I ask why not? It's obvious you're attracted to me." Duh, Ms. Obvious.

"Entanglements with residents are seriously discouraged, if not prohibited." She sounded like she was reading from a rule book.

"It wouldn't be an entanglement. I'm not a resident," I said, seeing an opening and jumping on the word.

"Then what exactly would it be?"

Faith had an expectant expression as she waited for my definition of what "it" would be. How do I say casual, convenient, temporary without it sounding like a simple, unencumbered hookup? And when did I consider a hookup bad? I struggled to find the right words.

"Do you have someone waiting at home?" God, that sounded corny.

"No."

"Someone on the ship?"

"No."

"Then it would just be two people enjoying each other's company. I'm single and unattached, and you just said you were—"

"And that means I'd be interested in being your vacation fling?"

"I will admit, I have taken advantage of…what I'd call…local opportunities," I said, finally finding the right word. "But that's not my intent with you."

"Well, you sure know how to make a girl feel desired," Faith said, half serious and half joking.

"Wow, I really stepped into that one, didn't I?" I said, shaking my head. "I mean, I did think about it, with you. What lesbian wouldn't? I mean you're gorgeous, funny, have a great smile."

"But?"

"I, uh." I stammered, not knowing what else to say.

"Then what exactly?" Faith shifted in the small seat to fully look at me, her eyes bright and large. "What exactly do you want, Ms. Carter?"

When Faith broke out the Ms. Carter, I knew I was in trouble. The moment on the trail was lost, and by the look on her face and the tone of her words, I seriously doubted I'd be getting another. I knew when to retreat and when to surrender. This was the former.

"I apologize, Faith. My mistake. I want to simply enjoy my time away from the office, and my parents, and if some or all of it includes you, then that will make it a very nice trip."

Faith looked at me for several moments, her expression unreadable. My leg started to bounce again, and I put my hand on my knee to keep it in place. I wished I could read her mind. What was going on behind those dark, curious eyes? Was she weighing the pros and cons of me? The risk to her job? If I was stable and not a crazy lady who would make her life miserable? Worse yet, display serious PDAs on the ship in front of her boss?

Before I could figure it out, she stood and lifted the microphone from the holder next to the driver, our conversation effectively over.

But I wasn't going to be deterred. I'd seen the look in her eyes, felt the slight tremor in her hand when she touched me. The heat between us was real, and I was not going to let her get away that easily. If fraternization was against the rules, then didn't the price of my parents' apartment carry some weight? I was going to find out.

# Chapter Thirteen

*Day Four*

"Ladies and gentlemen, our first stop this morning is Salamanca Place, which is one of the most popular tourist attractions in Australia." Faith was standing in the aisle, her microphone in her hand. Today she was wearing a pair of yellow shorts and a green and white tank top with the *Escape* logo. Her hair was in a ponytail, her sunglasses perched on top of her head.

"Large warehouses have been converted into restaurants, craft shops, and galleries. You can stroll through the famous Salamanca Market, where vendors sell fresh and gourmet produce, arts, crafts, and handiwork from all over the country. Get your shopping in because the market is open only today. And a bit of Hobart trivia..." Faith hesitated to let the suspense build. "Salamanca Place is featured as a property in the Australian version of Monopoly."

Faith looked at her watch. "It's now two fifteen, and the bus will leave from this spot at eight thirty. That's eight thirty," she repeated. "Please do not be late. We cannot and will not wait for you." Faith returned to her seat beside me.

"Have you ever left anyone behind?" I asked. I wanted to get the conversation between us going again.

"I haven't."

"What happens if not everyone is on time?" I knew the answer but asked it anyway.

"All the residents are responsible for themselves. If they aren't on board when we depart, we don't wait. We can't, because we have a schedule to keep. The ports where we dock are pretty busy, and we have an appointed time in and out. If we're late, one way or the other, it has downstream effects."

"No pun intended," I said. Faith looked at me blankly. I repeated my words, and when she frowned, I knew she had no idea what I was talking about. Even though Brits and Americans speak English, we sometimes don't speak the same language. "Downstream effects. We're on the water, the ocean, the ultimate stream destination." She still wasn't getting it. "Never mind," I said. I changed the subject. "Have you ever been to the market?"

"No, but if you can't find what you're looking for here, you probably can't find it anywhere."

The bus pulled into a crowded parking lot. "Looking for anything special?"

"Not really," she said curtly. "If you'll excuse me. Enjoy your day."

Faith resumed her duties, reminding the passengers of exactly when the bus would be leaving three more times, and had each of us repeat it as we stepped off the bus.

I'm not one for shopping, but the crowds had an energy and excitement that was contagious. The vendors were lined neatly in rows displaying their goods on tables, racks, and sometimes on a blanket on the ground. Everything was handmade, with bright colors and interesting designs and quality workmanship. The variety of goods was almost overwhelming, and the scent of fresh fruit was in the air.

Sensing I needed to back off, I followed Faith as she strolled the aisles. She picked up a few things here and there, spoke to several more vendors, and stopped at a tea cart, where she bought a cup of tea. Then she sat on a nearby bench in a beautiful green grassy area, her face to the sun.

❖

"May I join you?"

I wondered how long it would be before Lowe would approach me. She'd been following me for at least an hour.

"Of course." What was I going to do, tell her no? She was the number-one daughter of one of the richest residents on board. I knew better than that.

I didn't initiate conversation, even though I should have. It was my job, after all, to ensure that residents and their guests have the best possible experience. But I was still shaken by the almost-kiss yesterday and my reaction to it.

I'd tossed and turned most of the night, reliving the moment I almost let her kiss me. No, that was a cop-out. I wanted it to happen. I was going to let it happen. Making excuses was just that, an excuse. I didn't want to be responsible for my own actions, especially because I knew they were wrong. But how could something that felt so right be wrong? That sounded like a cliché, but it was true. We'd ended the day on what I would describe as an uncomfortable understanding that nothing was going to happen between us. If that was the case, why did I practically obsess over her all night?

"What are you drinking?" Lowe asked, finally breaking the long minutes of thick silence between us.

"Blueberry boost tea."

"Blueberry boost? A boost of what?"

"I'm not sure. It's made in Tasmania and is delicious." I handed Lowe the package I'd bought, turning it around so she could see the ingredients.

"It says it has spearmint leaves, raspberry and blueberry leaves, dried blueberries, hence the name, and cinnamon. Sounds delicious. It claims to balance albumin levels, whatever that is." She looked at me skeptically, then said, "It will lower your blood sugar, increase insulin tolerance, and improve your sleep. Wow." She handed me back the bag. "Delicious and good for you. Not many products can say that."

"If you're a tea drinker, you'll find a few stalls that sell different flavors, all made locally or from local ingredients," I said, just being polite.

The noise of the crowd and water from the fountain behind Lowe filled the silence between us. Tourists and locals strolled through the area, carrying bags of their purchases from the vendors. A toddler dressed in green shorts and a bright-orange T-shirt and sandals walked by, one hand holding his mother's, the other clutching a large apple he was sinking his teeth into. I couldn't help but chuckle.

"That apple is almost bigger than he is." I nodded in the direction of the boy. Sitting next to Lowe made me want to talk with her, share the experience.

"He almost needs two hands to hang on to it," Lowe replied, breaking into a big smile.

Silence fell between us again, this time a bit more comfortable. I found myself enjoying her company, even if we were just sitting and watching the crowds move leisurely from shop to shop.

"I apologize again for the other day. I was rude and presumptuous," Lowe said quietly.

She didn't need to be specific. "There is no need. We clarified the expectation."

"I don't want any tension between us."

"We're fine," I lied.

Lowe studied me for quite some time, as if waiting for my veneer to crack. It wouldn't, at least not in front of her. I had too much to lose. Finally, she looked away, and I started to breathe again.

"Would you like a refill?" she asked when I finished my tea. "I'm going to try it, and I'll be happy to save you the trip."

She looked at me so expectantly I couldn't refuse. I didn't want to either.

"That would be nice, thanks." She waved me off when I reached into my bag for my wallet.

"That's not—"

"I know. You forget my mother drummed good manners into me."

My heart skipped when she flashed me a smile.

By the time she returned with two very full drinks in her hands, I had regained some of my balance. How something as simple as a smile could knock the breath out of my lungs was frightening.

"Would you like to wander around some more?" Lowe asked. "There's a gallery a few shops down that Shirley was talking about last night at dinner."

I thought about saying no. I should have, but I found myself with absolutely no self-control. The last thing I needed was to spend a warm, sunny afternoon strolling through shops and galleries like lovers taking a break from loving.

We stopped inside the shop, and I was immediately drawn to a large abstract painting on the far wall. Lowe followed me, and I sensed her behind my left shoulder. I lost interest in the painting, my focus completely on the energy between us. It was palpable, and I knew Lowe sensed it as well. She took a half step closer.

"Lowe?"

I jumped, startled. Lowe stepped back.

"Hello, Mother."

"If I'd known you were going to be here, we could have come together."

I noticed Victoria approaching. Mrs. Carter still hadn't looked at me.

"There are some exceptional pieces in the back. Come. I'll show you," she ordered her older daughter.

I felt Lowe stiffen beside me.

"Mother, you remember Faith Williams from the *Escape*?"

I watched as Lowe's mother searched her memory to find me in her contact list and saw the instant she recognized me.

"Yes, of course," she said, but she made no other move to acknowledge me. Victoria, however did.

"You're the waitress, aren't you?" she said, knowing damn good and well I was. She was making a snotty point.

"Among other things, yes." My answer was clipped.

"I'm here with Faith, Mother. I'm sure we'll get to that part of the gallery. Thanks for mentioning it."

It was one of the smoothest shutdowns I'd ever heard. Mrs. Carter looked between me and Lowe several times. I knew she wanted to say more, but the expression in Lowe's eyes must have stopped her.

"Of course, dear. We'll see you at dinner."

I wasn't surprised when neither Lowe's mother nor Victoria said good-bye to me as they walked away.

"I'm—"

I held my hand up, stopping Lowe from what I knew was another apology for her family.

"No need," I said honestly. "You've already unnecessarily apologized once. You don't have to again."

"But—"

"No," I said firmly. "Let's just move on, shall we?"

We window-shopped and strolled in and out of the shops the rest of the afternoon. Lowe bought a few items for her staff, and I picked up a scarf for my mother and a crazy purse for Angelica. We snacked on ice cream in a bistro in the central square. The tension between us had dissipated, but the hum of desire followed us everywhere. If I had a normal life, this would be a picture-perfect day spent with my girlfriend. In a perfect world, one of us would be pushing a stroller occupied by a sleeping toddler. But I didn't have a normal life, and the world was far from perfect.

"We'd better be heading back," Lowe said, breaking into my fantasy. We'd had dinner at a quiet restaurant a few blocks from the market. "I hear the concierge from the *Escape* is ruthless and will leave anyone behind if they're late."

"I heard the same thing," I said, continuing the teasing. "She's a taskmaster and is solely responsible for ensuring that the ship departs on schedule." We were still sharing our private joke when the tender arrived at the ship.

# Chapter Fourteen

*Day Five*
*At sea*
*Hobart to Milford Sound*

"It's good to see you again, Ms. Carter."

A shadow floated over the tabletop, and I looked up into the smiling, friendly face of Captain Waverly. His uniform was gleaming white, and I shielded my eyes from the sun's glare.

"Thank you, Captain. Do you have time to join me for a cup of coffee?" I asked, indicating the empty chair across from me. I was enjoying my second cup of the delicious brew on the aft deck, my server hovering discreetly nearby.

"That would be nice, thank you."

As Captain Waverly sat, a bus boy placed a delicate cup and saucer in front of him. An instant later it was full of hot, black coffee.

"How have you been?" I asked. Captain Johan Waverly reminded me of the captain of the *S.S. Titanic*. His hair and beard were white and neatly trimmed, lines around his soft, caring eyes. I had never seen him in anything other than his immaculate white uniform. I had trouble keeping a pair of white shorts clean for more than an hour.

I'd read somewhere that he had over ten years of sailing experience on large cruise ships after a distinguished career as a commander in the British navy. His hat sat squarely on his head, the brim keeping the early morning sun from his hazel-green eyes.

"I've been well, thank you."

"And your granddaughters?" I asked.

The familiar sparkle came to his eyes as he gave me the rundown on his son's four daughters. We exchanged small talk for a few minutes when he asked about my trip so far and my excursions.

"Outstanding as usual. I spent the day with Faith Williams yesterday."

"How was the Airwalk? It is probably my favorite place in Hobart." He sat back and crossed his legs casually, his eyes scanning the deck for anything that needed his attention.

"Awesome. I'd recommend it to anyone. Faith was a fabulous tour guide. I know that's not her job, but she was very helpful and informative."

"I'll pass the compliment on to her."

We chatted for another ten minutes about nothing in particular as Captain Waverly finished his coffee. I wondered how many cups of caffeine coursed through his system on his rounds of meet-and-greet with his charges.

"Is there anything we can do to make your trip more enjoyable this year?"

I started to say no, but then a thought hit me. "As a matter of fact, there might be." I'd never asked for anything or taken advantage of my parents' resident position on the ship, but, hey, it was my vacation, and if I had to spend it with my parents, didn't I deserve a little reward?

## CHAPTER FIFTEEN

"Y ou bought me?"

Faith was standing in the hall, her hands on her hips, looking angry. I'd answered the insistent knock on the door while my parents and Victoria were finishing breakfast. I glanced behind me to make sure no one was coming to investigate Faith's raised voice, but the coast was clear.

"No, I didn't," I said, careful not to make Faith angrier.

"Then what *would* you call it?"

I fought the smile threatening to break across my face. She was kinda cute when she was pissed. "The captain asked if there was anything that would make my visit more enjoyable."

"And you said me."

I stepped into the hall and closed the door behind me. "Can we talk about this somewhere other than in the middle of the hall?"

Faith looked around, her expression falling. It appeared she'd just realized where she was and, unfortunately, who she was talking to.

"Come on," I said, taking her by the elbow and leading her to the outdoor terrace in the middle of the deck. Neither of us said anything until we'd sat.

"I am not a bonus that comes with the house payment." Her eyes burned, her words clipped.

"I know. You made that very clear before. I just mentioned to Captain Waverly that I enjoyed your company while we were in Hobart. He knows I'm here alone and asked if I'd like for you to accompany me on the excursions I had planned. It won't cost you anything. I agreed to pay for you."

"Now you really make me sound like a whore."

I couldn't tell if she was angry or hurt. Either way, her reaction was not what I intended or expected, for that matter. "If it upsets you so much, I'll go back and tell him no thanks."

"No," she said quickly. "That won't be necessary." Her voice quieted. "I apologize for my outburst. I didn't fully understand the situation."

Realization hit me that Faith actually believed she didn't have a choice. The mere fact that my parents owned one of the most expensive units on the ship entitled them and, by extension, their guests to anything they wanted. I felt ashamed that I had taken advantage just because I wanted to spend more time with her.

"You aren't under any obligation, Faith. If you don't want to do it or it makes you uncomfortable, then—"

"No. It's fine. No problem."

I think she was trying to convince herself.

"The purser will keep me informed of whatever activity you select. I'll be on the main deck fifteen minutes before departure time to go ashore."

"Faith," I said. She looked defeated, which was the last thing I wanted.

"Have a good rest of the day"

She got up and hurried down the hall, then disappeared into the stairwell. I started to follow her, to…what? Tell her how captivating she was and how she had completely fascinated me in the very short period I'd known her? That I wanted to know more about her? See her smile? Hear her laugh? Maybe feel her touch me? Yeah, right. That would make her feel at ease with her new assignment. I was still shaking my head when I returned to my parents' apartment.

"Who was that, Lowe?" my mother asked, as if anyone would dare solicit on their doorstep.

"It was Faith Williams," I said, assuming a nonchalant expression. "She's going to be my tour guide for the next few days, and we were just getting some of the details ironed out." That was one way to describe the last few minutes.

"I didn't know they offered private tours." Victoria's interest showed.

"I think this is just a one-time thing," I said, then changed the subject. The last thing I wanted was for Victoria to get an idea that she could have Faith as her personal escort.

❖

"Milford Sound, a fiord southwest of New Zealand's South Island, is within Fiordland National Park." I read from Wikipedia on my iPad screen in front of me. The sun was almost touching the horizon, the air chilly. I glanced at Faith, seated across from me at a small table on the back deck. Her polite expression had been there since she sat down a few minutes ago. It didn't take an astrophysicist to realize she was still angry. I'd wondered all day how long it would take for her to find me. I continued anyway.

"It's the world's top travel destination, according to an international survey, and is New Zealand's most famous tourist destination. Despite its name, Milford Sound is not a sound, but a fiord, the only one in New Zealand accessible by road. However, because it is bounded by steep cliffs and dense rain forest, its special features are unspoiled. Rain or shine, Milford Sound captivates even experienced travelers with its ink-dark waters, gushing waterfalls, and captivating views."

I pulled out all the stops to sound like an excited tour guide, including varying highs and lows in my speech cadence. It wasn't working. I switched to a different site.

"According to Trip Advisor, and I quote, Rudyard Kipling pronounced the breathtaking Milford Sound as the eighth wonder of the world. The star of glacier-carved Fiordland National Park, it provides an emerald-green, waterfall-rich backdrop for hiking, biking, and kayaking. Frequent downpours only enhance this South Island beauty, sending waterfalls cascading down the cliffs. Passionate nature lovers usually book in advance to hike the thirty-three-mile Milford Track, a legendary route through alpine passes and temperate rain forest." I wondered if there was a degree in brochure writing.

"Rudyard Kipling? Didn't he write the *Jungle Book*?" Faith asked from across the table. It was the first time she'd indicated she was listening with anything other than professional politeness.

"And *The Man Who Would Be King*," I added after reading one of the footnotes. I picked up a different brochure lying on the table in front of me.

"There's an underwater observatory." I read the information, this time to myself. I doubted Faith wanted me to continue reading to her. "This is interesting," I said, unable to keep my mouth shut. "It says the observatory is ten meters, under the Pembroke Glacier. That's about thirty-five feet for us non-meter citizens," I added, trying to inject some interaction between us. My attempt didn't appear to be working. "A layer of fresh water on top of sea water traps the light from getting too far past the surface and creates an environment similar to deep in the ocean, where we can see fish and coral and other deep-sea creatures we wouldn't be able to spot otherwise. Here," I said, handing the brochure to Faith. "It's like the opposite of an aquarium. We're stationary, and the fish swim around us. That's pretty clever."

My pulse kicked up when Faith took the brochure and studied it. Maybe she was interested after all. I wanted to spend time with her, but not if she felt like an indentured servant.

"I didn't buy you or your company," I said, putting the elephant on the table. "I enjoy being with you, and I thought the feeling was mutual." I hesitated a moment, an old, uncomfortable feeling resurfacing. "Or were you just being polite because it's your job?" I tossed back at her.

When I was growing up, and well into college, I was never sure if people liked me or my family's position, i.e. their money. They thought that knowing me would open doors that would normally remain closed, locked, and welded shut. They could meet the "right people" and gain entry into a world of wealth and, with it, power. I could further their career ambitions, position on the social ladder, or marriage prospects. Because of these possibilities, they never fathomed that I could also be a loyal friend—nonjudgmental, genuine, trustworthy, forgiving, dependable—a great listener, and accept them just as they were.

My entire life everyone had deferred to me because of my family. I'd gotten out of that cruel, superficial atmosphere when I separated myself from that life. I'd worked hard to be me, not a descendent or recipient of something I didn't earn. A thought occurred to me, and I chuckled.

"Obviously you think this is humorous," Faith said, tossing the brochure onto the table and crossing her arms over her chest.

"Actually, I think it's more ironic than humorous," I said flatly.

"Please share, because at the risk of losing my job, a job I love by the way, I don't see this as either."

I had to admit Faith was pretty brave putting that out there in the universe. "The only thing I ever wanted was to be seen for me, not my parents and not for how much money others thought I had. What's ironic is that here, on the *Escape*, I can't."

Faith frowned, obviously not following my statement.

"I'm on the *Escape* and can't *escape* from it." I sighed heavily and dropped back into my chair, realization surrounding me like a thick, dark cloud. It was smothering.

The silence between us was uncomfortable. I stared into the rolling waves of the Tasman Sea, looking for answers but knowing they wouldn't just jump out of the water and into my lap. My life had never been that simple, or that whimsical. Reality became crystal clear as the sun peeked out from the clouds overhead.

"Forget it," I said, gathering up the brochures and flyers of excursions. "It was a bad idea. I'll let Captain Waverly know that I changed my mind."

"No," Faith said, but I interrupted her.

"Don't worry. I'll make sure he knows my decision has nothing to do with you or your willingness to go along."

"I'd like to see the observatory. It looks interesting."

I looked down into Faith's eyes, judging if her statement was for real or more of the deception life too often tossed my way. Her eyes were direct, focused on mine, and unwavering. I wanted to trust her, *really wanted* to trust her. At the risk of being disappointed, or worse yet, hurt again, I asked, "What time would *you* like to leave?

# CHAPTER SIXTEEN

*Day Seven*
*Milford Sound, New Zealand*

What had I gotten myself into? I'd agreed to, what? Accompany Lowe everywhere she went on her vacation? Be her travel buddy? Personal tour guide? I'd been furious with Lowe when Jacobs told me. I'd thought, how dare she assume I was available for her own personal use? The gall of her to presume I'd want to. I was still apprehensive about what was involved in this arrangement, but after I calmed down and thought it through, my gut told me to do it. Raul, however, sensed it was something else, and he'd called me on it last night.

*"What's got your girlie boxers in a wad?"*
*Raul was sitting across from me as I stabbed at my dinner on the plate. Raul, a twenty-eight-year-old Cuban, was my gay BFF. At six foot, four inches, he was taller than most Cubans, and a birth defect had left him with four fingers on each hand. We'd met during new-hire orientation and had instantly hit it off.*
*It was after six, and I was still hot about my new assignment. I'd been stunned, then furious after Jacobs, the captain's executive officer, informed me that, how did he phrase it, "You've been assigned to Miss Lowe Carter for the duration of her visit." I wasn't sure if the expression on his face was a sneer, a look of envy, or his belief that I'd been purchased.*

*"Captain Waverly pimped me out to Lowe Carter."*

Raul coughed, choking on his water. *"He what?"*

*I told him of my conversation with Jacobs, then my idiotic confrontation of Lowe.*

*"Wow. All I did was fold sheets all day."*

*One of the perks of being a resident was the twenty-four-hour laundry service.*

*"What are you going to do?"*

*"Keep my mouth shut and my map handy."*

I'd thought about Lowe all night. She was unlike any resident, or very rich person, I'd ever met. When others were pompous and self-important, Lowe was kind, humble, and unassuming. I'd heard stories confirming how my peers were treated like little more than the hired help, which I had experienced as well. Lowe, however, treated everyone with dignity and respect. My friends and colleagues who had come in contact with her couldn't stop raving about her.

Maybe she was different? Maybe she was exactly as she seemed to be—honest, caring, and interested in the people around her. I had to admit I was attracted to her. Jesus. I'd almost let her kiss me. But that was not going to happen again.

I hurried to finish dressing because I wanted to be on deck as we approached the fiord. I'd done my own research on our port of call, and even though I was still hesitant about what the day would bring, I was excited to see the towering, sheer-granite walls, waterfalls, and lush greenery.

It was early, and I was alone as I stood at the very tip of the bow. I'd secured my hair at the base of my neck, but the strong breeze had tugged a few strands free. The air was chilly, and I was glad I'd pulled a light jacket from my closet before leaving my room. As we approached, the sun was starting to peek out from the horizon, the first morning rays painting the cloudless sky in a blaze of colors. I was lost in the splendor of the exploding sunrise and didn't hear Lowe approach until she stopped beside me. An overwhelming sense of calm and tranquility instantly settled around me. The stillness of the dawn was filled with a complete sense of rightness. We stood silently shoulder to shoulder until the bottom edge of the sun cleared the horizon.

"It was beautiful, wasn't it?" Lowe's words were quiet, as if she was referring to the pristine sunrise.

I simply nodded.

"Would you like some coffee?"

"That would be nice. Thank you." We still hadn't looked at each other.

"I'll be right back," she said, slowly turning away as if reluctant to leave.

Lowe returned a few minutes later with two tall white paper cups of coffee. She handed me one, and I was careful to grasp it around the thick, heat-resistant sleeve. Our fingers touched, and a jolt of electricity shot through me. I looked up and met piercing blue eyes smoldering so hot I had to look away. If I didn't, I'd fall into them and never want to find my way out.

"Thank you," I managed to say. My hands were shaking, and I wrapped both of them around the cup, hoping to not spill the hot contents all over myself. I sipped, the liquid almost scalding my tongue.

We didn't sit or move away from the railing as we drank our coffee while the ship slowly maneuvered into the fiord. We'd lay anchor in the spectacular channel of Milford Sound, the actual dock too shallow for the big ship. Then we'd be tendered ashore.

The sun was well into the early morning sky when I finally found my voice. "We'd better get moving if we want to catch the boat to the observatory. It leaves at eight thirty."

Lowe didn't move, and neither did I. It was as if we both wanted the serenity of the sunrise to last all day. We had a lot to do in the next twelve hours, but we didn't seem to be in a hurry to do it. Actually, it didn't seem that we were in a rush to do anything. And I didn't care.

We boarded the ferry a little after eight with several chatty couples and a few crew members. My peers were whispering among themselves, a few daring to look at Lowe and me several times. I was uncomfortable but knew we weren't doing anything against the rules. Their expressions told me they thought otherwise.

The water in Harrison Bay was clear and calm, the glacial mountains grand and beautiful. Water cascaded down the mountain amid the tropical landscape. It was a scene worthy of any Hollywood movie. We arrived at the observatory, and Lowe and I were the last to disembark. She politely reached out to help me navigate the floating dock, and a surge of warmth made my arm, and other parts, tingle.

A guide met us just inside, where we learned about the history, geology, and wildlife in Milford Sound. At least I think that's what he was saying when he pointed to some information on large, colorful panels behind him. I was too distracted by Lowe standing close to me. When she shifted to see a monitor showing a video of a local avalanche, our arms touched, sending a wave of excitement through me. I glanced at Lowe, and she appeared not to notice until I saw the vein in her neck pulsing rapidly. Mine followed suit.

We descended into the observatory, the space expectedly small and dark. Lowe was behind me, and I felt her body heat as we maneuvered through the tight crowds. In one area, she pressed up against me when a large man pushed his way through the crowd behind us. She had her hands on my hips to steady us, and an image of them sliding around in front of me flashed through my mind. Against my better judgment, I leaned back against her. It had been a long time since I'd felt another woman's body against mine, and with my growing attraction to Lowe, I had little willpower to stop myself. Lowe shifted, her arms encircling me. Her breathing quickened. My head started to drop back, giving her access to anything she wanted. But a toddler squealed, and I jerked up.

I jumped out of Lowe's arms and stepped away, my legs shaking. I didn't dare look at her. If I did I'd be swept back into that reckless moment. I exhaled deeply, my checks puffing out as I shook my hands to regain control. Jesus. I really had to get over this insanity and pay attention to what was going on in another place than between my legs, or it was going to be a very long trip. The crowd thinned, and I put a more respectable, less tempting distance between us. I didn't look at her.

We made our way back outside to wait for the ferry. Other than the normal small talk and comments about the fish and coral in the observatory, we hadn't said anything since I stepped out of her arms. Lowe turned to me several times to say something, but I shut her down. I didn't want to talk about it. I wanted my attraction to her to just go away.

"Faith," Lowe said, and I almost gave in. The sound of my name, the deep tone of her voice was almost enough to make me abandon common sense again.

"I don't think we have time to do anything else today," I said quickly, not giving her a chance to go where I didn't want her to. "By the time we get back to the *Escape,* it'll only be a few hours until we depart."

I turned to Lowe when she didn't answer. She was frowning, her expression intense. I could see she was debating with herself as to whether she should push the subject or let it go. At least that's what I'd be doing if our roles were reversed. I wouldn't let Lowe get away without clearing the air between us or kissing her senseless. I wanted the latter but had no idea what she would do.

Lowe's eyes roamed every inch of my face, returning several times to linger on my lips. My heart was pounding, and I was sure Lowe could hear it. I was barely able to control my breathing and tried my hardest to appear calmer than I felt.

"I suppose you're right," Lowe finally said.

Somehow, I knew she was agreeing only to my comment about the time.

# Chapter Seventeen

*Day Nine*
*Akaroa, New Zealand*

I was up early and, from the privacy of my patio, watched as we docked in Akaroa at eight that morning. I hadn't slept much the past two nights, and I kept remembering the stricken look on Faith's face as she stepped out of my arms at the observatory. It was bad enough she didn't want anything to do with this arrangement, and after the clinch in the dark, I felt guilty for putting her in this position. What had started out as an opportunity was now anything but. It was somewhere around one in the morning when I decided I'd make this the best experience I possibly could for her. She might feel like she had to accompany me, but I was going to make it as enjoyable for her as it was going to be for me.

Akaroa, the guide had told us last night in the briefing, is a village a little more than seventy-five minutes from the more famous city of Christ Church. "Akaroa means long harbor," the bald man explained. "It was named best cruise destination in Australia and New Zealand in the Cruise Critics' award in 2017," he read off a piece of paper in his hand. We're here for two days, enabling us to tour the galleries and craft stores, enjoy a hot stone massage, or play a round of golf on their famous mini-golf course. All those activities sounded a bit too boring, so I'd signed up for kayaking and possibly an hour on a jet ski. I passed on the Alpaca Farm Tour.

Faith was waiting for me on the main deck when I stepped out of the elevator. She was wearing a pair of jade-green shorts with a light-green tank top and a pair of water shoes. She held the same bag she had carried in Hobart and had a death grip on the Nike visor in her hand. We exchanged polite greetings, then took the elevator to deck five, where a ferry would take us to the dock.

Two men with almost identical neatly trimmed beards helped us onto the worn, weathered dock. One of the men was much taller than the other and had an accent so strong I could barely follow what he was saying. Thankfully, he didn't talk much.

We bounced along a steep, narrow road in a caravan of four-wheel-drive Jeeps. The scenery was magnificent, with green rolling hills. There were eight of us, three couples, Faith, and me. There was only one single kayak, so I offered to double up with Faith. We were fitted with compact life vests and a paddle, and after fifteen minutes of instruction, we were ready to slide our bright-yellow kayak into the water.

Faith was up front, so she climbed in first, her position giving me a perfect view of her fine ass as she maneuvered into the tight seat. Once she was settled, I did the same, but certainly not as elegantly as she had. We dug our paddles into the sand and pushed off into the water.

Our guide took us along the outer coast of the Pohatu Marine Reserve, where we paddled through narrow passages of towering rocks that jutted into the clear blue sky. The water was crystalline, providing an excellent view of the reefs below and some very colorful fish. I pointed out a colony of seals sunning on a large rock in the distance to Faith. Passengers in another kayak exclaimed when they saw several dolphins in the area.

"Did you know that Pohatu is home to the largest penguin colony in New Zealand?" I asked, trying to impress Faith with my odd snippet of obscure information I'd read on one of the many websites last night.

"I didn't know that," she replied over her shoulder.

I couldn't tell if she was impressed.

"You can sign up to spend the night in their colony," I added. Not my idea of an enjoyable time, but if Faith wanted to, I'd be curled up behind her. I wasn't surprised when she said she wasn't interested.

We were on the water about ninety minutes before we dragged our kayaks out. Our guides pulled out a cooler from the back of one of the Jeeps, and I took an ice-cold bottle of water and leaned back against a rough rock, Faith nearby.

We chatted about the excursion, and I sensed her mood shift as she described how some of the fish were chasing each other. I'd love to chase her until she caught me, I thought.

Our rest break over, we squeezed back into the Jeeps to begin our ascent back to the pier.

"How about a jet ski?" I asked, pointing to several of the watercraft pulled on shore. A sign sticking out of the sand gave the price list. It was early afternoon, and we still had several hours of daylight left before the ferry returned to the ship.

"After that quiet, tranquil, calming experience, you want to ride on a jet ski?" Faith looked at me like I'd lost my mind.

"Come on. It'll be fun." I started walking in the direction of the little guy in the bright-green hat who was manning the booth next to the sign. I waved my arm, not giving her much chance to decline. That was my plan. She'd been on guard all day, and I just wanted her to relax and have some fun.

Ten minutes and a hundred bucks later, I had settled behind Faith, my legs straddling hers, my arms around her waist as she hit the throttle. I'd purposely let her drive because I'd yet to forget how good it felt with our bodies pressed against each other. Life was good. If we didn't have on such bulky life vests, it would be close to perfect.

## Chapter Eighteen

*Day Twelve*
*Auckland, New Zealand*

"We're climbing it?" I asked Lowe, my head tipped back so far I almost fell backward.

A fear of heights was rapidly rising in my throat. We were at the base of the Auckland Harbor Bridge, an eight-lane box-trussed bridge over the Waitemata Harbor.

As a child I'd climbed onto the roof of my house and couldn't get down. It was forbidden to climb the large tree in our neighbor's yard, but Max Cargill had dared me one boring summer day.

I was generally a rule follower, but Max had been after me for weeks. Finally, after one name-calling too many, I shimmied up the big tree. I was going to show the neighborhood bully I was not to be messed with, so I scooted along a crooked branch and dropped onto my roof. I had just turned around to gloat in my accomplishment when my pop pulled into the drive.

After he went inside, I knew I'd better get my scrawny butt back on the ground before I got caught. He wasn't mean or abusive, but he did expect the rules to be followed. Max, being the chickenshit he was, ran into his house, leaving me like a castaway on an island. A very high island. I carefully retraced my steps to the branch and was shocked when getting back onto it was impossible. The first time I tried, I lost my footing and barely caught myself from falling two stories to the ground. I didn't try again.

I was on the roof in the hot Florida sun for over an hour. My mother thought I was next door with Max and didn't expect me home until dinner. Max knew I was stuck up there and, a few minutes later, even went so far as to wave at me from his bedroom window, the little jerk.

Finally, my pop came outside, and I had no choice but to call for help. I was so scared he had to carry me down the ladder.

"I hear it's a must-do in Auckland," Lowe said, excitement in her voice.

It was, but I wasn't sure I was up for it. The top of the bridge was two hundred feet above the water, and you ascended to the top of the bridge secured to a specially engineered catwalk. Lowe wasn't Max Cargill, and I felt no pressure to go. I also felt safe with her.

"Let's do it," I said firmly to convince myself.

After a thirty-minute safety briefing and donning the required climbing gear, we followed our guide to the first stop on our climb. He pointed out the safety features of the bridge and its engineering history and answered dozens of questions from our fellow climbers.

I stayed close to Lowe, trying not to panic myself into embarrassment. I felt safe next to her, as if she could save me if I started to fall.

At the summit, the view was stunning. The sky was clear, offering a stunning view of Auckland. It was windy, making conversation difficult, but nothing I could have said could describe the thrill of the climb or the beauty of the country from that view. Lowe was equally silent, as she had been when we shared the sunrise. Our guide snapped our picture before we descended.

Along the way, we stopped at a platform specifically designed for bungee jumping. We watched for a few minutes as a man in a harness prepared to jump. When he did, he screamed the entire time.

"Are you the adventurous type?" Lowe asked, coming up behind me.

"Absolutely. You?"

"Wouldn't miss it," she replied, her smile amusing.

My stomach tickled. "Let's go then."

Once again, I found myself trussed up in a harness attached to what looked like a giant rubber band. Lowe and I were jumping together, so we were also attached to each other. We stepped out onto the platform, and Lowe grabbed my hand.

"Ready?"

I nodded. We jumped.

I think we both screamed as we fell toward the water below. While other jumpers chose the full dunk, we elected to fall far enough to touch the water before we were yanked up. We gently bounced up and down several times before we were lowered to the deck of a pontoon boat.

"Oh my god," Lowe said, hugging me. We'd had an exciting, mind-blowing experience. "That was freaking awesome."

My adrenaline was still pumping, and all I could do was nod in agreement. My stomach was still somewhere in my throat.

Back at the base of the bridge, Lowe hailed a cab to take us back to the *Escape*. We chatted like excited teenagers, clasping our photos in our hands. I had had more fun than I could have imagined with Lowe, and when she invited me to dinner instead of returning to the ship, I couldn't refuse.

The taxi dropped us off at a quaint restaurant on the bay. We were seated on the patio, and when our after-dinner wine arrived, the lights on the bridge were ablaze.

"Beautiful, isn't it?" our waiter asked, pouring the wine.

"Absolutely." I meant both the light show and the entire evening with Lowe. She'd kept the conversation going, entertaining me with stories of ridiculous customer demands. She laughed when I shared some of the more interesting things I'd seen people do in places the *Escape* had stopped.

We sipped our wine, comfortable with the silence between us. I kept telling myself this was not a date, but it sure did feel like one. We were two lesbians sitting across from each other at a table covered with a white tablecloth, a candle in the center flickering in the dim light. Soft music came from somewhere, and the waiter was attentive but discreet.

"We should be getting back." I didn't want to leave, but we had only an hour to get to the ship. An erotic thought crossed my mind of what might happen if we missed the departure.

Lowe, sighed, her disappointment apparent. "I suppose so," she said and signaled for the check.

We rode back to the ship in silence, and Lowe took my elbow as we got out of the cab. We started walking toward the ferry gate, but Lowe pulled me aside into a shadow and took my hands in hers. My pulse skipped, and I knew she was going to kiss me.

"I had a wonderful time this evening."

There was enough light for me to see the smoldering look of desire in her eyes. It was strong, and I wanted to melt into it.

"I did too." My heart was still beating fast from the entire evening, and when she tipped her head toward mine, the world stopped.

I was stunned when, instead of kissing me, Lowe kissed the back of each of my hands. Her lips were warm and moist, and when she withdrew, I felt just a hint of her tongue. Her gesture was gracious and gallant and made my stomach tickle.

"The whole day was wonderful."

# Chapter Nineteen

*Day Fourteen*
*At sea*
*Auckland, New Zealand to Great Barrier Reef*

I tied my bow tie, my reflection in the large mirror clearly showing I hadn't put on enough sunscreen the last few days. We were halfway through our three days at sea and would be arriving at the Great Barrier Reef the day after tomorrow. My nose was sunburned, and you could see the distinct outline of where my sunglasses had been all day. My mother had, of course, not approved but mercifully hadn't said anything about it.

She had reminded me no less than three times about the diamond jubilee celebration that the Cobalt family was throwing for their parents tonight. They had invited all the residents on board and most of the staff as well. I had reluctantly packed for the occasion. It wasn't as if I minded dressing up. I often attended various charity functions, but I didn't look forward to my mother's comments and disapproval of my choice of formal wear.

I knew the Cobalts and spent time with them on my visits. They were a genuinely warm and friendly couple, obviously just as much in love today as they were sixty years ago. They both were physically frail but mentally still very sharp.

I would spend a few hours in the afternoon with Mr. Cobalt sitting by the pool or on the atrium deck. I was usually reading a business journal, he working a crossword puzzle from the thick book he habitually had in his lap. "Crossword puzzles keep the mind sharp," he would say, and I believed him because he did them in ink. A few days ago, I'd made it a point to stop by their apartment and thank them for inviting me to the party. The Cobalts have four children, twenty-seven grandchildren, and, at last count, eight great-grandchildren. The guest accommodations on the *Escape* were limited, so only his children and their spouses would attend. I knew the Cobalts had probably spent more than a small fortune getting their family here. If my parents ever had a celebration like this, it would be a more private affair, and I was certain the only staff in attendance would be the wait staff.

I thought about the conversation I'd had with my mother this morning. We were seated at the table, a plate of muffins and assorted fresh fruit between us.

*"You've been spending quite a bit of time with one of the members of the crew."*

*I'd just finished my first cup of coffee. I knew what she was really saying because I'd heard it my entire life. It was her "disapproving yet trying to not show it" voice.*

*"I see a lot of people while I'm here."*

*"Yes, I know, dear. But I've heard you're spending an extraordinary amount of time with Faith Williams."*

*A spark of anger flared in my chest. I didn't like the way my mother said Faith's name. She could have very easily said, "that woman."*

*"She's my tour guide." I didn't want Faith to appear to be something she wasn't. "And your point is?" I asked when it was apparent that was my next line.*

*"I'm not sure if that's a wise thing to do."*

*"And why is that?"*

*"Well, she's...".*

*"She's what?" I prompted my mother.*

*"She's a member of the crew."*

*"And what's wrong with that? She has a job, just like I do. There's nothing wrong with working here, is there?"*

"But that's different," my mother said. "You don't need to work."

I clenched my jaw so that I wouldn't blurt out what was on the tip of my tongue. I'd never considered selling myself out to live off money I hadn't earned. A view completely lost on my parents. Instead I said, "And how do you know Faith isn't in the same position?"

"Because she's working here."

"So? I work in a pack-and-ship store."

"That's different. You own the store."

"I see," I replied. This was a status thing, a class distinction. Before my parents moved onto the *Escape* I had wondered if their life on the ship would help or hurt their disjointed view of the world. It had gotten worse.

"And how do you know she doesn't own this ship, or the cruise line?"

"Don't be ridiculous, Lowe," my mother said dismissively. "She..."

"I'd be very careful how you describe her," I warned her, my undertone clear.

"I'm just saying that she works here. What could you possibly have in common?"

*More than you'll ever know*, I thought.

"What will happen when we arrive back in Sydney? When you go home?"

For the last few days I'd wondered the same thing. Every other visit I'd literally counted the days down until I was able to leave. Since meeting Faith, I counted the days until I was scheduled to. "I don't know, Mother, but I think that's between Faith and me."

My mother's eyes flared. She didn't like to be challenged, and she certainly wouldn't be happy if I had a relationship with Faith.

"I just think it would be difficult for both of you," my mother said, adjusting her tone, evidently hoping to appear she was simply offering sage advice to her eldest daughter.

"I appreciate your concern, Mother but I'm thirty-six years old, and I know what I'm doing."

*Silence stretched out between us, and before too long my mother asked, "You did bring something appropriate to wear to the Cobalts' anniversary party, didn't you?"*

*Her question irritated me, not only because she asked it but the way she phrased the question and her tone. Everything always had a negative connotation. "You did bring something appropriate, didn't you?" versus "what did you bring to wear to the party"?*

I put on my jacket and slid my room key, a credit card, and some cash into my pocket. Then I counted to ten before I stepped out of my room. I'd made a wager with myself on how long it would be before my mother or Victoria commented on my suit. Less than a minute, I was thinking. Judging by Victoria's expression when I stepped into the living room, I knew I had grossly overestimated the length of time.

"My god, Lowe. You look like a man."

"Thank you, Victoria. I like what you're wearing too. It's a good color on you." I didn't even attempt to hide the sarcasm in my voice. "Vera Wang?"

Victoria squinted and then grasped the undertone in my compliment. It was not a flattering look on my baby sister.

"I certainly don't know what you do at home, but do you think that's appropriate to wear to an event of this magnitude?" She waved her hand at me like she had something stuck to her fingers. Obviously, Victoria thought the party was the equivalent of the coronation of Prince William as the new King of England.

"Clearly I do. And yes, it is quite nice, isn't it?" I looked down at my perfectly tailored tuxedo. "There's a specialty shop in Phoenix that carries the ladies' line of Armani," I said, as if name-dropping the expensive designer would solve the issue. "I was able to get it pretty much right off the rack." That was a bit of an exaggeration. I'd had the sleeve lengthened by a half inch and the trousers taken in an inch at the waist. Nothing would irritate and gall Victoria more than to think I'd walked in off the street and bought something for such a special and visible event. I doubted that Victoria ever bought anything that she didn't have altered, whether it needed it or not. I was certain she had specially ordered her jade-green, knee-length dress for this occasion.

"Hello," my mother said from behind me.

When I turned, I was certain my mother hadn't recognized her own daughter standing in her living room. "Hello, Mother. That's a beautiful dress." My compliment was more out of habit and politeness than the fact that it was beautiful. It was too pale for her complexion, and the sequins on the floor-length dress made it much too formal. But I knew not to question her or voice my opinion if it was anything other than positive. I'd learned long ago to keep my viewpoint to myself.

"This is what Lowe is wearing to the party," Victoria said in a tone that she used to get me in trouble when we were children.

"Lowe, do you really think—"

"Yes, Mother, I do." I quickly cut off the objection I knew would follow. I refused to change, not only because I didn't have anything else, but because there was absolutely nothing wrong with my attire for the evening.

The thick tension in the air between us was finally broken by my father when he stood up and rubbed his hands together.

"We need to go," he said, not even looking at his watch. "We don't want to be more than fashionably late."

He barely glanced at the three of us, but his eyes lingered on me for a split second longer, and he frowned.

I stepped into the hall and waited for him to lock the door behind us. Victoria and my mother didn't. They practically stomped down the hall, anger seething from them.

I stood next to my father in the elevator, the mirrored doors reflecting just how much I looked like him, especially in formal wear. We had the same cheekbones, blue eyes, and chin. My father's hair was gray and thin in a few spots, and I remembered him being taller than he appeared now. My mother's forehead was still creased in disapproval, and Victoria scowled as we rode down to the main deck.

The doors opened, soft music and murmured voices greeting us as we stepped off the elevator. I surveyed the room, nodding a greeting to several familiar faces. More than a few reacted similarly to my mother and sister when they saw what I was wearing. *Jeez. Get over it, people.*

It was crowded, a quartet of musicians seated on a temporary platform next to a stage in front of the room. The music blended with the tone of the occasion. The women wore dresses in various colors and lengths, but all the men wore basic tuxedos with a white shirt and black tie. From a distance, my tuxedo looked black, but it was in fact a deep shade of blue, my silk tie also blue with white polka dots. It wasn't one of the premade ties that clipped on, but an authentic bow tie, and I'd spent hours in front of a mirror learning how to tie it perfectly.

A plump woman in her mid-sixties wearing an unflattering, rust-colored, floor-length gown, her hair piled neatly on top of her head, approached, an expectant expression on her lined face.

"Francis, Landon, thank you so much for coming. My parents will be thrilled."

My parents returned the greeting, my mother giving the woman a polite air kiss. "These are my daughters, Victoria and Lowe."

Whereas most parents introduce their children in birth order, mine did just the opposite. It had ceased to bother me, as I understood where I stood in the familial pecking order.

"This is Madeline Miles, Franklin and Josephine's eldest."

"Thank you for coming," Madeline said, shaking Victoria's hand.

"Thank you for inviting us," Victoria said. She definitely knew how to play the social game. "We've heard so much about your parents. They sound like wonderful people."

Madeline turned toward me. "I'm sorry. Lowe, did you say?"

I extended my hand. "Yes, Lowe Carter. Pleased to meet you, Madeline."

"So you're the infamous Lowe Carter," Madeline said, blatantly appraising me suspiciously, and it clearly wasn't what I was wearing that she disapproved of.

I saw my mother shoot her glance at me. No one wanted their child to be infamous. Famous yes, infamous, no.

"Well, I don't know what I did to earn that designation, but I do know your parents, and they are absolutely wonderful."

"Yes, and you are as well, according to them. They seem to be quite smitten with you, especially my father."

A harshness in her tone put me on guard. Did she actually suspect I was after something from her parents? I pitied her if she thought that.

"I visit them every time I come on board," I said, keeping my tone light. "Your father and I work the crossword puzzles."

"Yes," Madeline said, looking me over, not even bothering to hide her rudeness. "He says you are quite helpful to him."

"I wouldn't categorize it as that. I come up with a four-letter word now and then when he needs it," I said, staring directly into Madeline's eyes and daring her to continue this absurd train of conversation. She got my message

"Well, thank you all for coming," Madeline said, stepping back and effectively granting us access to the room. "Mother and Father are around somewhere. Please stop by and say hello. My siblings will introduce themselves throughout the evening. Please help yourself to the buffet and cocktails. We'll be having a toast at nine thirty."

Victoria stepped up, obviously designating herself as the speaker of the family. "Thank you, Madeline, we will. It's a lovely evening for the celebration."

"I got the impression Madeline doesn't care for you," Victoria commented after the tight-ass, pompous woman walked away.

"Really?" I asked, my question fake. "I have no idea why she wouldn't. Her father and I are nothing more than casual acquaintances. Now, if you'll excuse me, I'm going to mingle."

I disappeared into the crowd, incensed from Madeline's ridiculous innuendoes. I hoped she hadn't said anything to her father. He was a sweet man, and I enjoyed talking with him. He had never been anything other than a complete gentleman every time we were together.

Beer wasn't a selection at the bar, so I ordered a cocktail and scanned the crowd, looking for Faith. She hadn't mentioned if she'd been invited, but I'd seen other crew members in attendance in formal wear and had overheard others talking about their invitation to the party.

I left a hefty tip on the bar, and the bartender extended a sincere thank you. I always tipped generously. He would certainly remember me next time, and there definitely would be a next time.

I stepped away from the bar and heard my name called from my right. Shirley was waving at me, and I started in that direction then stopped suddenly. Faith was standing next to her, stunning in a simple black dress that fell just below her knees. Her hair was up in a French braid, sparkling earrings dangling from her ears. The cut of her dress was simple and elegant, held up by thin spaghetti straps across her shoulders. Polished toenails peeked out from the end of very tall, strappy sandals. Her dress fit her perfectly, accentuating her curves and bringing out the tan of her skin. Breathtakingly beautiful, she was the only thing I could see, my view completely focused on her. My heart pounded, the beat deafening. My mind raced at the image of her dress slowly sliding off her shoulders and falling in a pool at my feet. I wondered what she wore underneath.

Someone bumped me, jostling me out of my sexual stupor and propelling me in their direction.

"My goodness, Lowe," Shirley said as I approached. "You look so handsome, if I may say so."

"Thank you," I replied, forcing myself to look at Shirley. After all, she was the one speaking to me.

"If I were thirty years younger, I would hope you would ask me to dance.'

Her statement surprised me. "Age is only a number, Shirley, and I would be honored to dance with you. Save me a place on your dance card?"

"Absolutely," she said." Don't wait too long. I go to bed early, you know."

I turned to Faith, and my mouth was suddenly very dry, all of the blood cells needed for my brain to have a normal conversation rocketing southward. Faith's eyes burned, taking what little breath I had recently refilled in my lungs. She wore little makeup, and what she did have on accentuated her eyes, her glossy lips an invitation to be kissed. I pocketed that enticement for later.

"Faith, you look lovely tonight." I moved near, fully intending to buss her check, but when the scent of her perfume hit me, I leaned in closer and whispered, "You're absolutely beautiful." I felt Faith's sharp intake of breath and stepped back, pleased that she was equally affected by our encounter.

"Thank you," she replied, her face flushed.

"Doesn't Lowe look dapper? It's the only word I can think of," Shirley said.

"That's not the word that comes to mind," Faith murmured. "But it works."

My pulse raced even faster, the pounding between my legs growing harder at Faith's innuendo.

"Where do you get a tuxedo that fits like that?" Shirley asked.

I felt the heat of Faith's gaze as it skimmed over my body. "At a specialty shop in Phoenix."

"May I?" Shirley asked, reaching out and touching my sleeve. "My goodness, this is very nice." She moved her hand over the fine material. "And I don't think anyone else in the room could carry off that tie," she said, pointing to my collar that suddenly felt too tight.

"Feel this, Faith," Shirley said running her hand down the sleeve of my jacket. "This is quality."

Faith reached out and moved her fingers under the lapel of my jacket, the back of her fingers skimming my breast. I didn't forget to breathe. I simply couldn't. The nearness of Faith and her soft touch drove every thought from my mind except taking her to a very private place and finding out exactly what was beneath that dress.

Faith's eyes shot to mine, and I didn't even try to hide my desire. What was the point? Hiding it wouldn't get me where I wanted to be, which was naked with Faith.

"Oh, there's Tom," Shirley said, breaking the connection. "If you two will excuse me," she said, not really asking our permission.

I put my hand over Faith's before she could remove it. I pressed it tighter against my chest so Faith could feel my pounding heart.

My back was to the crowd, so I wasn't worried that anyone would see what I was doing. For an instant, I didn't care if they did.

"My god, you are beautiful," I said, the word insufficient to describe Faith this evening.

"Thank you," Faith said, her voice just above a whisper.

Still pressing Faith's hand against my chest, I leaned in again. "Do you want to get out of here as much as I do?" I slid Faith's hand under my jacket. There was no way she could miss the hardness of my nipple or my message.

❖

My heart throbbed and my head spun, and if Lowe hadn't been holding my hand, I would have dissolved into a hot mess on the floor. I knew Lowe had been invited to the party, Mr. Cobalt telling me as much the other day. I'd been nervous ever since and had rummaged through more than a few of my workmates' closets for something appropriate to wear. In the end, I settled on the dress that had been carefully wrapped in the back of my small closet. You just can't go wrong with basic black. I'd borrowed my shoes, however, from my hall-mate, Donna, who just so happened to be heading our way, her eyes wide.

Reluctantly, I pulled my hand from Lowe, instantly missing the connection.

"Faith, there you are. I've been looking for you all over."

I knew Donna was lying. She'd waved to Shirley and me just before Lowe joined us. She wanted to meet Lowe, and this was her not-so-subtle way of accomplishing just that. Lowe gave me one more burning look before turning her attention to Donna.

"Donna Evans, this is Lowe Carter, Mr. and Mrs. Carter's daughter," I offered for introduction.

"Miss Carter, pleased to meet you," Donna said, appraising Lowe like she was the dessert tray.

"Please call me Lowe."

"You're visiting your parents?"

"Yes, I am."

"How long are you staying?" There was more than polite conversation in her question.

Jealousy shot through me, equally unintentional and ridiculous. If Donna wanted to have a shipboard fling with Lowe, that was her business. But I'd never get over it if she did.

"I'm scheduled to depart when we return to Sydney," Lowe replied, then glanced at me. My skin tingled. "But I may stay longer."

"Wonderful," Donna said, still holding Lowe's hand. "Would you like to dance?"

I was stunned at the boldness in Donna's approach. I looked at Lowe, unsure what her reaction would be.

"Actually, I promised the first dance to Faith," she said, smoothly withdrawing her hand from between Donna's. "Maybe some other time."

Donna looked back and forth between Lowe and me, her eyes laced with anger. "Yes," she said. "Maybe later."

How interesting that Lowe had committed to dance with Shirley but had shied away from an obvious opportunity with Donna, who was obviously offering more than a round on the dance floor.

## Chapter Twenty

D ance with me?" Lowe asked, holding out her hand.

I hesitated, and Lowe said, "You wouldn't want me to look bad, would you?"

Lowe was a probably a good dancer, but I had never danced with anyone who had physically affected me as much as she did. I'd probably stumble over my own feet and make a complete fool of myself. I could barely think, let alone form a complete sentence when I was this close to Lowe, so how in the hell would I be able to put one foot in front of the other? More appropriately, one foot behind each other.

After a rocky start the first morning in Milford Sound, we'd gotten along much better than I expected. Lowe was casual without being overly so, and I knew she was making an effort for me. At the end of the day, I'd grudgingly admitted I'd had a wonderful time.

Not coming up with an appropriate excuse not to dance with her, I placed my hand in hers.

"I certainly wouldn't want to be the cause of making you look bad." I was surprised at my ability to be flippant when my body was betraying me.

I felt dozens of eyes on us as we walked hand in hand to the center of the dance floor. When Lowe stopped and pulled me into her arms, I thought I heard a gasp or two from behind me. Lowe didn't appear to have heard it, nor did she seem to be the slightest bit uncomfortable if she had.

I stepped into her arms and almost stumbled at how perfectly we fit together. Her arms were strong yet held me gently, a respectable distance between us. She smelled delicious, and I inhaled her scent several times.

I tried to make conversation, when all I wanted was to settle against her and turn off the world. I felt safe, warm, and protected.

"Shirley was right. You do look very handsome."

Lowe smiled and my heart flipped.

"My mother thinks my choice of formal wear for this evening is appalling."

I slid my hand from Lowe's shoulder, down her back, and up again, feeling the texture of her jacket. The softness and quality of the material was unmistakable, and I told her as much. I didn't share how much her muscles reacting to my touch affected me.

"Oh, it's not what it's made of. She just thinks I should wear something that shows off my legs and my shoulders."

I couldn't help but laugh at Lowe's sense of humor. "Really? Would she think it more appropriate if you had on a pair of knickers and a tank top?"

Lowe laughed, a deep rumbling in her chest that caused a shiver to traverse through me. It was a wonderful sound, and I needed to think of ways to make her laugh more often.

"That probably would be worse," Lowe said, still chuckling.

"Well, I think what you're wearing is perfectly acceptable. You look better than any woman in the room." I leaned back a little, taking another opportunity to look her over. My heart was in a race with my pulse for beating the hardest.

"Thank you," Lowe said, her smile showing that she appreciated the compliment.

"My sister almost had a stroke, and my mother didn't even recognize me standing in the middle of her apartment. I'm sure she was tempted to ground me for the evening."

"And what did your father think of his daughter looking so dashingly handsome tonight?"

"You think I'm dashingly handsome?" Lowe asked while looking at me, her eyes twinkling.

"Absolutely. In an unthreatening kind of way. I like it." It was true, and I didn't want to deny it.

Lowe's eyebrows rose at my descriptor.

"Very much so," I added for emphasis. The look in Lowe's eyes made me thankful for my new job. "What about your father?" I asked, desperate to chase erotic thoughts of Lowe out of my head.

"He didn't say much. My father is a strange guy," she said, frowning. "Most of the time he's exactly like my mother, but he bails out and heads to the golf course as much as he can. I think that's his coping mechanism. Neither one of them gets me. What about you?" Lowe asked, shifting the conversation away from herself. "Does your mother get you?"

Dozens of images of my mum "getting me" flashed through my head. She'd sit on the sidelines watching me play softball before her overnight shift, when more than likely all she wanted to do was be home in bed catching a few more minutes of sleep. She'd done without, so I could play a musical instrument in junior high. And she looked so proud when I told her I'd been offered the job on the *Escape*. But my most vivid memory was her reaction when I told her I had a girlfriend instead of a boyfriend.

*It was late Friday night when I returned home from a high school football game my junior year. That in and of itself wasn't unusual, though what was had changed my life that night. I had kissed Michelle Miles behind the science building. Obviously, it was a kiss like none other I'd had before, and, in that instant, I knew I would never kiss another boy. I'd come home, shaken from the experience. I tried to disappear into my room to relive it repeatedly, but my mum evidently knew something was up and called me into the kitchen.*

*I was never able to keep anything from her and certainly wasn't able to lie to her, so when she asked what was wrong, I blurted out everything, starting with "I kissed Michelle Miles." My mum's expression didn't change as she processed the information and what it meant. The longer she didn't say anything the more nervous I became, until finally tears started rolling down my cheeks.*

*My mum reached for me and held me tighter than I could ever remember. She smelled like coffee, cookies, and hairspray, three things that remind me of her even today.*

*"Faith," she said, her voice muffled by my head in her bosom. "I don't care if it's the man in the moon or the woman of your dreams that makes you happy. All I want is for you to be happy. That's all I have ever wanted."*

*My mum's reaction surprised me. She'd always been open-minded and accepting of everyone, but it was different when your own daughter tells you she's a lesbian—very different. But not my mum. She was wonderfully supportive, and we spent the next hour talking about my feelings for Michelle. I went to bed clinging to her final words. "Just be careful, Faith. There are people out there who will hurt you because of this."*

"Yes, she does," I replied simply. My mum is an uncomplicated woman, no frills, pretense, or exaggerations.

"As it should be," Lowe said. "I think it's the parents' job to raise children to be respectable, honest citizens independent of them. Kids grow up and move out of the house for a reason. My administrative assistant once said that you teach your children to be thoughtful and have their own opinions, beliefs, and ideas, and then you have to bite your tongue when they do. My mother got the first part of that message, but not the second."

"Yet you come visit every year?" I said, then instantly regretted my question. "I'm sorry. It's none of my business." I was so comfortable with Lowe it seemed natural to ask.

"No. It's okay. They're my parents," Lowe said, as if it were a no-brainer. "They have idiosyncrasies, weird habits, and some ridiculous beliefs, but they're still my parents, and I'm their child. They won't be around forever, and if visiting them gives them a little bit of joy in their life, then so be it. What about your mother? How often do you see her?"

"Not as often as I'd like," I replied, unable to keep the sadness from my voice. "It's difficult because I travel all over the world, but I see her as much as I can."

"Does she ever come here?"

"She's been on board once, but only for a few days. It's hard for her to get away."

"She must be very proud of you."

"I think so. At least she tells me that all the time."

"What about your father?" Lowe asked carefully.

"My birth father was never in the picture. And my stepfather died when I was twelve." Just thinking about my pop made me remember the way he used to laugh all the time and play games with me and kiss my mum every time he left the house and when he came home. "But, as you know, the ship has Skype and the internet, so there are lots of ways to stay in touch."

"But it's not the same."

"No, it's not. But it won't be forever, and my mum knows that."

Lowe looked over my left shoulder. "Your friend Donna is shooting daggers at you."

"That's all right. I'm wearing Kevlar."

Lowe's eyes narrowed. My breath caught at the heat directed my way.

"Where?" she asked, looking at my dress. "No, wait," she said. "Let me just imagine."

I flushed everywhere Lowe's eyes traveled, and I felt like the most desired woman in the world. I memorized everything about this evening.

I wasn't surprised that Lowe was an excellent dancer. She was tall and strong, and she telegraphed her moves with a subtle squeeze of my hand or light pressure on my back.

Her scent and being in her arms was intoxicating, stirring and making me crazy. It was so easy to get lost in the music, the feel of her arms around me. Every negative thought, worry, and problem dissolved as we glided across the dance floor. An unfamiliar warmth started in my midsection, slowly spreading to my limbs. I felt like I was floating, the bonds of responsibility nonexistent. I could get used to this, I thought as Lowe expertly maneuvered us through the crowd. A few heads turned as we passed.

"May I cut in?"

The familiar voice of Raul brought me out of my fog.

Lowe looked at me for confirmation that it was okay to let him step in.

"Thank you for the dance," I said, even though I didn't want it to end. Lowe gallantly stepped back and allowed Raul to take her place.

"Lowe, this is Raul Diaz, a good friend of mine. Raul, Lowe Carter."

"Pleased to meet you, Ms. Carter, and thank you." His accent was heavy as he thanked Lowe for letting him cut in. Lowe gave me another long look before turning and walking toward the bar.

"What in the fuck are you doing?" Raul asked in Spanish as soon as Lowe was out of earshot. He had started teaching me his native language shortly after we met.

"I beg your pardon?" I said, my accent flawless.

"You heard me, *chica*. Are you out of your mind? Everybody, and I mean everybody, is watching you two make goo-goo eyes at each other. For God's sake. You both should be stark naked by the way you're undressing each other."

"We were not." I started to defend myself, but Raul cut me off.

"Think again, sister. Better yet, get a room. On second thought, if you keep this up, you may need to find a new job." Raul's eyes were dark, his tone serious.

"We're not sleeping together," I said firmly. Not that I hadn't thought about it constantly and dreamed of it just last night. Many naughty images flashed in my mind.

"Hello?" Raul asked, snapping his fingers in front of me. "Earth to Faith."

"What? Oh, sorry," I said, the heat of embarrassment on my face.

"I can only imagine where you went, but I know who you were with. And don't tell me you don't know what I'm talking about." Raul maneuvered us around a pair of kids dancing. "One more minute down memory lane, and you would have embarrassed yourself."

"One more second is more like it," I said, breathing deeply to try to clear my head.

"You've got it bad, girl."

"No shit, Sherlock," I shot back. "I mean, look at her," I said, doing just that. Lowe was standing next to the bar talking to one of the residents. She looked so good it hurt. "She oozes sensuality." Raul swung me around so he could see Lowe.

"Even I think so, and I don't drink out of that glass," Raul said.

"What am I supposed to do?"

"Stay away from her."

"That's not as easy as it sounds. I'm with her almost every day."

"Then just do it."

I stumbled at Raul's blunt statement.

"You heard me. Drag her into a very private place and fuck her brains out. You know where they are." Raul was alluding to the private and some not-so-private places for intimacy. They were well-known secrets, at least with the crew. "Just do it and get her out of your system," he said, this time in English.

I laughed at his reference to the Nike tag line. It helped me get my feet back on solid ground, or floating wood floor, to be precise. I dropped my forehead against his.

"What am I going to do?"

"I already gave you my opinion, and judging by the look on that woman's face," Raul tipped his head in Lowe's direction, "she's in complete agreement."

I lifted my head and met Lowe's eyes across the room. Even from this distance, I could see they were hot and burning. So much for getting under control, I thought.

"Faith is such a wonderful girl, isn't she?" Shirley asked a few minutes into the song. I had stepped away from the temptation of taking Faith in my arms again and had asked Shirley to dance instead.

"Shirley, I'm not going to talk about another woman when I'm dancing with you. It's rude."

"Baloney," Shirley said, tapping my lapel. "You're not my type, but she is."

"That may be but—"

"But nothing. I've learned many things in my life, and the most important is that life is too short. If you don't go after and grab what you want, someone else will. And you'll regret it the rest of your days."

"It's not like that. Faith is—"

"Hot for you.'

I stopped, causing a couple to shift quickly to avoid running into us.

"I'm old but not blind. She doesn't let you out of her sight. She lights up when she sees you."

During the rest of the dance, I focused my attention on Shirley, but I'd kept one eye on Faith most of the evening. She danced with a few people, and every trip to the bar was to refill her glass with Coke.

Madeline nabbed me the instant after I returned Shirley to her table.

"I see you're having a good time." Madeline sounded disappointed.

"Yes, I am, very much so. It's a wonderful celebration." I flagged down a passing waiter and took a glass of champagne from the tray. "I spoke with your parents. They're so happy you're all here."

"We're a tight family. We watch out for each other, especially our parents."

Madeline's words contained no lack of innuendo.

"From what I've seen, they're both really sharp and deeply in love."

"Yes, for now. But there will come a day when that's not the case, and we want to make sure no one takes advantage of them." Her message was clear, and she obviously didn't care about the love part.

"Your parents are lucky to have a family like yours. I'm sure they'll be fine."

A protective feeling crept into the back of my neck, and I searched for Faith. A man I didn't recognize in a blue suit was standing too close to her for my comfort. She was backed into a corner and didn't look happy about it.

"Excuse me," I said, not waiting to see the expression on Madeline's face and not caring.

I grabbed a glass of water from a tray held by a crew member who had obviously not been invited to the party.

"There you are," I said, stepping next to Faith. "Here's your water you asked for. Sorry it took so long," I said, not knowing how long Faith had been talking to the man. He turned to me, the unmistakable odor of alcohol on his breath that matched his glassy eyes.

"Have we met? Lowe Carter." I used the introduction to step between them.

The man looked at me, trying to figure out if I was a man or woman. I was used to his reaction and recognized the confusion no matter how good the person was hiding it.

"Lowe, this is Daniel Barber," Faith said, maneuvering out of the corner. "He's married to Paula, one of the Cobalts' daughters."

Piece of crap is what he is, I thought. Hitting on another woman during the wedding-anniversary party for his wife's parents. I hoped he'd fall overboard in his drunken stupor.

"Marshall said he'd like to talk to you," I said, my attention shifting from the sleazy bastard to Faith. For a few seconds, Faith looked confused but then caught on.

"Oh, good. I've been looking for him."

"I'll take you to him. Excuse us." I grasped Faith by the elbow and led her away before the man had a chance to object.

"Thank you."

"You looked like you needed rescuing."

"Yes and no. But thank you anyway. He was quite persistent."

"So was Madeline."

"The Cobalts' daughter? What was she persistent about? No. Wait. Don't answer that. It's none of my business." Faith held up both hands, palms up.

"It's okay," I said. "She warned me that she and her family were watching out for their parents."

"Watching for what?"

"That someone doesn't swindle them."

"Like who?" Recognition quickly dawned on Faith, and she asked, "You?"

"I guess my being polite and visiting them is a sure sign I'm after their money."

"That's ridiculous."

"Well, Madeline doesn't think so."

The warm ocean air greeted us as we stepped outside. The sky was clear, the stars brilliant against the night sky. By unspoken agreement, we'd left the party, and Faith led us to the sundeck at the rear of the ship.

"This view never gets old," Faith commented when she stopped at the rail. The noise of the party dimmed with each step away from the door.

I could barely see the wake churned up by the big ship as it motored through the water. I stopped close beside Faith, resting my left hip against the rail.

"It's beautiful," I said, my observation directed at both Faith and our surroundings. A moment passed before she turned and faced me. The sliver of a moon reflected off the water and onto Faith's face. She was breathtaking.

"I can think of only one thing better." We were only a few inches apart, and I felt Faith's breath hitch when she saw the desire in my eyes. Anticipation is the best aphrodisiac.

Faith's eyes locked with mine, then dropped to my lips. She wanted me to kiss her, and I was more than willing to oblige. An instant before our lips met, I hesitated. My heart hammered, and my pulse jumped a dozen beats a second. I had never been so ready to kiss a woman.

"Kissing a beautiful woman under the stars."

I lowered my head, slowly, savoring every moment. The instant before our lips met, Faith licked her lips. My heart raced faster.

Faith's lips were softer than I'd imagined, and I wanted to spend hours tasting them. Neither of us moved to get closer or deepen the kiss. I was overwhelmed with sensation, every nerve alive, attuned to her. She smelled like lilacs, and her lips, molding and responding, tasted like berries. Nothing existed but the two of us and the night.

I was the first to break the kiss, my breathing fast and shallow. I was dizzy and needed Faith to ground me. I opened my eyes and found Faith's searching mine. Was she looking for the same explanation of what had just happened to me? Was she astonished at her response to the kiss? Did she want to do it again? Feel my lips on her skin? Taste every warm, wet inch of me? Run back to her cabin alone or take me with her? Did she want to spend the hours till daylight lost in my embrace, needing more and more and more?

That was exactly what I wanted, and I was paralyzed, afraid I'd push Faith too fast or not fast enough. Decisions ruled my life. I made dozens every day, some impacting millions of dollars and affecting more lives than I was comfortable with. I knew when to take a woman to bed and when to simply take her home. I knew when to stay for breakfast and when to leave in the middle of the night. I knew when to call or never to leave my number. I could always determine if the woman wanted romance or a quick, mind-blowing fuck.

But I was completely out of my element with Faith. The overwhelming need for her both exhilarated and frightened me, and for the first time in my life I was almost paralyzed with fear. I was afraid if I did the wrong thing I'd lose Faith or I'd lose myself.

"I've wanted to do that from the moment I saw you," I finally said, my voice husky with desire.

"I'll bet you say that to all the crew members that run you down on your first day on board."

Faith's breath caressed my lips, and I wanted, no, needed to kiss them again. "Only the ones that take my breath away with their beauty and make my heart race when they smile."

Panic flashed in Faith's eyes. "I have to go," she said quickly, stepping away from me.

"Faith, wait," I said as she started to walk away. "I didn't mean to upset you."

"It's not that. I just need to go."

"I'll see you to your room," I said, not wanting our evening to end but respecting her need for it to. I didn't understand. Her signals were as strong as mine, but I refused to press her.

"That's not necessary. You go back inside."

I started to protest that I would never not walk my date to her door, but Faith stopped me.

"This is not a date, Lowe, and I'm all over this ship by myself all the time. This is no different. Go back inside and enjoy the party."

Before I left her, I was determined to have one more kiss. I cupped her face in my hands, letting my fingers tangle into her hair. I tipped my head toward her and gently kissed the corners of her mouth. It was sweet, and I almost disregarded her words and whisked her into a dark corner. When I pulled away, we were both breathing heavily.

"This is much more than a date."

## CHAPTER TWENTY-ONE

*Day Sixteen*
*Great Barrier Reef, Australia*

I woke the next morning in anticipation of spending the day with Faith. It was going to be a beautiful day of sun and snorkeling at one of the seven wonders of the world, the Great Barrier Reef. I hadn't slept much last night, memories of Faith invading every sense as I walked away from her on the fantail. I'd had to clench my jaw so hard, I thought I'd break a tooth as I put more and more distance between us only because she asked me to. Her lips were as soft as the finest silk, her kiss sweeter than honey, but it held the promise of much, much more. Faith had piqued my interest unlike anyone had in a long time, if ever.

I pulled my tank top over my head, not even bothering to check if it messed up my hair. I rarely looked in a mirror, and when I did, it was never to fuss with my hair. Cutting it this short was one of the most liberating things I'd ever done. Sometimes I thought I did it because it was completely against the wishes of my mother and the disdain of Victoria, but I'd grown used to it and really liked it. More heads turned now than ever before, which was also quite okay with me.

I made my bed, even though I didn't have to. Felice would be in later today to straighten up. Other than JulieAnn, who came in once a month for heavy cleaning at my house, I didn't have anyone to clean up after me. Though my parents thought it was beneath them to perform such a menial chore, I didn't.

During my last visit, Felice had fussed at me several times, telling me that making my bed was her job. Her argument didn't sway me then, and it didn't now, so I plumped the accent pillows before tossing them toward the headboard.

I slipped my feet into my deck shoes, grabbed my bag and checked that my towel, sunscreen, and snacks were inside, and headed to the kitchen. Victoria and my mother were sitting at the table, a delicate coffee cup on a saucer in front of each of them.

"Good morning," I said, opening the cabinet and reaching in the back for a sturdy mug. I preferred them over the delicate cups and handles that my fingers barely fit in. I was waiting for one of them to mention my dancing with Faith last night.

"Where are you off to today?" Victoria asked.

It was one of Victoria's more stupid questions. We were at the largest coral reef in the world with thousands of colorful tropical fish and beautiful beaches.

"Snorkeling."

"Don't you know all that sun will ruin your skin, Lowe?" my mother asked.

My back was to her, and I rolled my eyes as I poured my coffee. I replaced the carafe and sat down beside my sister. "Yes, Mother. I'm aware of that. I think I'll be fine." I knew it was a mother's job to mother, but for crying out loud, enough already. Then again, Francis wasn't being a mother. She was being controlling.

"Did you get a new suit?" Victoria asked.

"No." I saw my mother look at my swim shorts with a critical eye, searching for a stray thread or any sign of fading.

"You know you really should stay on board and visit," Victoria said.

I sipped my coffee, paying particular attention not to slurp. That would definitely garner a very unfavorable look from my mother.

"Visit with who?"

"Visit with whom." My mother corrected me.

I wasn't sure who was right.

"With your family," Victoria replied, like I'd asked the dumbest question ever.

"We visit all the time," I countered. "And when we do, we don't have a lot to talk about. We don't have similar interests, and we all have our own separate lives."

"And that's my point, Lowe," Victoria said. "We see you only once a year, sometimes less. We want to be more involved in your life, and you should be more involved in Mother and Father's."

I kept my face expressionless. That was the second time the subject of my family wanting to know more about my life had come up on this trip. It was two times more than they had ever inquired about it. What was really going on?

"Well, you've asked some questions, and I answered them. But you didn't like some of my answers," I added, reminding them.

"Since when do we have to ask?"

"Since you've never been interested before," I said without thinking. I looked at my clunky waterproof watch. I had ten minutes to get to the main deck.

"Lowe, you know that is not true," my mother said, soundlessly setting her cup on the matching saucer.

"As much as I'd like to discuss this, I have to go. We can pick it up later this afternoon when I get back. Or this evening over dinner?" I suggested, dumping the remnants of my cup into the sink. Then I put it in the dishwasher—another of Felice's jobs.

"I should be back around four. What are you two going to do today?" I asked out of polite habit. It wasn't that I didn't care what they did. It was just that their interests were so diametrically different than mine, I'd learned from my mother how to fake interest.

"We have an appointment in the nail salon, and I need to get my hair touched up." Victoria patted her hair as if I had no idea where it was.

I looked at it critically and didn't see anything that needed "touched up," but then again, what did I know about hair? Mine was the same color as when I was born, and when the gray started coming in, it stayed.

"Okay. Have a good time. See you this afternoon." I grabbed the bag I'd dropped by the front door and headed out, imagining my mother and sister shaking their heads. They had no idea about me just as I had none about them. How three people could be related and be so different always amazed me.

Arriving on the main deck, I carefully opened the stairway door. Several people in swimwear were milling around, and Shirley was struggling with her beach bag. She lost, its contents spilling onto the tile floor.

I stepped forward, my foot stopping a container of sunscreen rolling toward me. I picked it up and walked toward her. "Let me help you with that." I scooped up a few other items and handed them to her.

"Thank you," she replied, sounding truly grateful. "I don't know why I always bring more stuff than I could possible need."

"That's because you have everything anyone else could need," I replied, hopefully putting Shirley at ease at the numerous contents of her bag.

"My husband would always shake his head at the size of my bag. But when he needed something, he always turned to me."

We chatted a few more minutes, and I kept one eye on Shirley, with the other watching for Faith. I was excited about seeing her in a swimsuit. I didn't care if it was a string bikini or a skin-tight wet suit. Each offered a different view of what had to be a dynamite body. When it came to clothing, I liked more rather than less, giving my imagination the chance to work on what was hidden underneath. Half the fun was the discovery.

"There's Faith," Shirley said, looking over my left shoulder. "She looks so cute in that outfit."

Cute was not the adjective I would use to describe her as she walked toward us. A bright-orange sarong was tied around her waist, the top of her suit peeking out from under a white tank top. Matching orange flip-flops with some sort of geometric design on the top straps were on her feet, her toenails painted to match. Her hair was up in a tight bun, accentuating her high cheekbones and dark eyes, a bright-green beach bag with a yellow sunflower on the side hanging from her shoulder.

Faith hesitated for a moment when she spotted me. Obviously, she too remembered last night. I felt the warmth of her eyes as they traversed up and down my body. I worked out when I could and needed to, but I wasn't going to starve myself to look like what other people thought I should. Sure, I could probably look better if I tried harder, spent more time at the gym, and ate better. But I was comfortable, and that's all that mattered. Especially when I saw Faith's appreciative look.

"Faith." Shirley waved, motioning Faith to join us.

"Good morning," Faith said, more to Shirley than to me.

"I was just telling Lowe, my bag is always overstuffed with more things than I could possible need. Are you working today?" Shirley asked.

Faith shot a quick glance at me before answering. "No. Actually, I have the day off."

"Wonderful," the woman said, clapping her hands together. "Then you can simply enjoy yourself."

"Yes, well, I'm never really off duty." Faith shot me another glance.

"Well then, let's get going," Shirley said, taking Faith's arm and turning her toward the door.

The dock was busy, people scampering here and there trying to find their boat. I was the first to see the sign for slip 52. The vessel was sparkling white, with a royal-blue mast, *Windstream* stenciled in big black letters on the bow. Several people were in line to board, a member of the crew checking paperwork as they stepped forward.

"Good morning, ladies, welcome aboard." A grizzled, fifty-something man with long gray hair greeted us. His teeth were far too white to be original, his skin leathery. I knew he hadn't listened to his mother about sunscreen. He put a checkmark by our names on the clipboard he held and introduced himself as Captain Nate.

Faith boarded first, and from my vantage point, I could watch her butt sway with each step, one of the most arousing and quintessential elements of femaleness. She had a small geometric tattoo just below her hairline on the back of her neck. I'd have to ask if it held any special significance. I took a leap and thought it probably did. Faith didn't seem the type to do anything on a whim. Maybe I could change that.

"You two go on," Shirley said. "I'm going to sit with Joyce."

"On top okay with you?" Faith asked, pointing to the top deck.

"Absolutely." I replied to the same question but with a very different meaning. Top, bottom, front, back—it all worked for me.

Her butt was right at eye level as we ascended the stairs. It was as firm and perfect as any I'd seen in years, and I was tempted to take a bite, or a lick. I quickly glanced around to judge the likelihood of being observed. All I needed to do was reach up and...

"Stop looking at my ass," Faith said without ever turning around.

How did she know that was exactly what I was doing? Did she have eyes in the back of her head? The thought was intriguing. What would I see in them as I rode her ass to climax?

"Shit." I knocked my shin on the step in front of me. It was covered in thick rubber for slip resistance, but the blow hurt nonetheless.

Pay attention, Lowe, and stop slobbering over her like a sex-starved teenager, I told myself. The teenager was more than two decades ago, though the sex-starved hadn't been that long ago. But just looking at Faith made that stage of my life seem like much, much longer.

As I hit the top step, the early morning sun blinded me from any more innocent but very arousing views of her backside. I shielded my eyes and followed her to two empty chairs in the first row.

I dropped my bag, but when Faith leaned over to set hers on the deck, I caught more than a glimpse of smooth, brown curves. I knew I shouldn't stare, but I'd lost my manners somewhere after we boarded.

"Are you a good swimmer?"

"Excuse me?" I said, catching only the last few words of Faith's question.

"Are you a good swimmer? You'd better be, because if you don't start paying attention to what you're doing, you might fall overboard and drown." She cocked her head in that cute get-a grip-I-know-what-you're-doing way.

"I'd rather pay attention to what you're doing."

"That's pretty obvious," she said, shaking her head but not able to hide a small smile.

Every woman is beautiful in her own way, and ego aside, it just feels good to know someone thinks you are. I was sure Faith had no shortage in that area. Her dark hair was made to slide fingers through, her bare skin to float across like a caress begging to be kissed. Expressive eyes that saw everything and could read into your soul needed to be ablaze with passion and desire. "Whoa there," Faith said, snapping her fingers in front of my face. "Cut it out. You're starting to embarrass me."

"Sorry," I said, but really wasn't. "I'll behave."

"I doubt it, but I'd appreciate it if you'd try."

"No, really, I can," I said quickly. *Yeah, who am I kidding?* "Can I get you something to drink?" I had to change the subject. The more you try not to think about something, the more you do.

"Water would be nice, thanks."

"I'll be right back." Without the distraction of Faith's ass, I smoothly scampered down the steps I'd stumbled up a few minutes ago.

A continental breakfast was laid out on large trays across a counter, and I filled one plate with an assortment of fruit, the other with pastries. Tucking two bottles of water under my arm, I hurried back to the top deck.

Faith had removed her tank top and added a pair of sunglasses, and now she was pulling her hair through the back of a white cap. Believing she couldn't see me, I stood silently and watched as she secured her hair, the movement raising and lowering her perfect breasts.

"I know you're there."

Shit, busted. It must have been my heart pounding that gave me away.

"Breakfast is served," I said, pretending I'd just stepped onto the deck and hadn't been gawking again.

I placed the overflowing plates on a small table in front of us. When I handed Faith a bottle of water, our fingers touched. A line from the Tina Turner song *What's Love Got to Do with It* played in my head. It was something about how the touch of her hand makes my pulse react. That and other things as well.

I had it bad. I either needed a cold shower or a hot woman. Unfortunately, for the next six hours, my options involved lots of strenuous activity, and I didn't mean for two.

"Who are you feeding?" Faith asked, pointing to the plates.

"I didn't know what you liked, so I got a little bit of everything." I named off the fruit and muffins like she'd never seen either. Anything to keep my mind off imagining a very different breakfast—one in bed after a night of passionate sex. I kept my face innocent, my thoughts anything but.

"Thank you. That was very thoughtful."

I wanted to say I always aim to please a beautiful woman, but "you're welcome" came out of my very dry mouth.

For the next thirty minutes, others joined us on the top deck, and one very attractive, very attentive deckhand hovered nearby. She looked barely out of her teens, but there was nothing girlie about the way she filled out her bikini. I couldn't help but think about what her mother would say about all that delicate skin exposed to the harsh rays of the sun. She introduced herself as Bethany and said she was here to help make our trip as enjoyable as possible. I glanced around and saw several of the men had their eyes glued to the girl. I could only imagine what was going through their heads minutes later as they watched Bethany bend over and untie the line that secured the boat to the dock.

Captain Nate's voice boomed over the speakers, introducing himself again, along with his crew. After giving a brief safety talk, including the location of the lifejackets and instructions on what to do if someone fell overboard, we were on the way. Captain Nate skillfully maneuvered the boat through the crowded channel out to the open water.

We'd been underway about thirty minutes when Faith tilted her head toward Bethany. "She seems very concerned that you have a good time today."

"It's her job. I suppose they work for tips." Bethany had been flitting around every few minutes asking if I needed anything and making small talk.

"Well, she's working for something else."

I turned to Faith, expecting to see a green cloud of jealousy over her head. Obviously, there wasn't one, but I certainly heard it in her words. Butterflies fluttered in my stomach. Maybe she wasn't as disinterested as she seemed.

"She's not going to find it here," I said honestly. Sure, I was aware of the girl's clichéd drop-dead gorgeous body and her obvious willingness to hook up, but I wasn't interested. I would probably spend the rest of this trip celibate and have Faith only in my dreams. As much as I needed release caused by a pair of hands other than my own, I don't think of someone else when I'm with someone. Faith slid her sunglasses down her nose and appraised me over the top of them. I could sustain her scrutiny because what I'd said was true.

We weren't traveling very fast, and I sat back and simply enjoyed the view with Faith beside me. The hum of the engine and the rhythm of the boat through the water was relaxing.

My dark sunglasses were perfect for girl-watching, and I took full advantage of gazing at Faith stretched out across from me. I knew she'd caught me staring more than once, and I was sure she knew I was watching her, but I didn't care. There was no point in hiding my attraction to her. We were well past that.

A very tall, very thin woman approached and introduced herself as "Anne with an *e*." Anne had spent way too much time in the sun and way too little at the dinner table. She stopped beside Faith.

"Good morning, ladies." She had an Irish accent. "Are any of you interested in doing SNUBA today?"

I'd read about the opportunity yesterday in the brochure next to the sign-up sheet. SNUBA is a cross between snorkeling and scuba diving yet requires no previous diving experience or certification. The diver uses fins, mask, and a weight belt to explore underwater.

Instead of air tanks attached to the diver's back, the tanks are on a small raft that remains on the surface. The air hose is twenty feet long, allowing the diver to move around underwater freely but not go any deeper. I looked to Faith to decide for us. It sounded interesting, but I wasn't going to leave Faith alone for a minute.

"I would, yes," she said, not even looking at me. I guess she didn't have the same desire.

"Count me in," I said, and Anne with an *e* took our names and told us we would be the second group to go down. We'd have time to snorkel beforehand. She walked away but not before handing us each a clipboard with a small stack of papers attached.

"Ever been?" I asked

"Yes," Faith answered. "Have you?"

"Nope. I'm a SNUBA virgin."

"Then I'll tell her to be gentle with you," Faith said nonchalantly as she filled out her paperwork.

"I'm a big girl. I think I can handle just about anything this trip throws at me." Except Faith, as it was turning out.

The sun warmed my skin as the boat motored through the water. I counted at least eight other boats already anchored along the reef.

Bethany came around handing each of us a face mask and snorkel and asked for our shoe size. Several minutes later she returned with her arms full of yellow rubber fins. She asked if I needed some help with mine, but I assured her I could figure it out. She walked away seeming disappointed.

"Hi, girls."

Shirley approached and sat down next to Faith, and some of the tension between us dissipated.

"I've never done this." She looked more than a little nervous.

"I'm sure you'll be fine," Faith said.

"Oh, I will. I'm going with the beginning group. We'll have someone with us all the time."

Shirley started to put her fins on.

"You put those on when you're in the water," Faith said, and Shirley chuckled in embarrassment.

I'd have loved nothing more than to spend the rest of the day sightseeing with Faith, but Shirley was a sweet woman with a wicked sense of humor. She was also a good buffer between Faith and me. As Faith laughed at Shirley's attempt to adjust her mask and snorkel, I had an excellent opportunity to watch her without being rude and creepy.

I knew it was the job, but it appeared that Faith was genuinely interested in Shirley. The times I'd seen them together, Faith was attentive and focused on Shirley, who, in turn, reveled in the attention. I hoped that when I was Shirley's age, someone as young and beautiful as Faith would equally enjoy my company.

## CHAPTER TWENTY-TWO

The boat slowed as we approached a small island with a sandy shoreline. As I stood and untied my sarong, I felt Lowe's hot eyes on me. My pulse kicked up, my heart skittered, and my mouth went suddenly dry. I tugged off my sunglasses, stowing them in my bag before turning to Shirley.

The engine stopped, and a deckhand wearing a face mask and a pair of green fins grabbed a yellow rope and dove off the bow. He swam deeper and deeper to secure a line to an anchor on the ocean floor. Bubbles trailed the man as he exhaled during his ascent back to the surface. I heard a second splash from the stern and assumed that another deck hand was securing the opposite end to keep us from spinning in circles.

Captain Nate's voice came over the loud speakers giving final instructions, including specific ones to stay at least five feet from the delicate coral and not touch any fish.

I gave the crowd a few minutes to clear the boat before descending into the water, amazed it didn't sizzle from the heat coming off me.

I swam away, fully aware Lowe was watching me. I hadn't been able to see her eyes, but I knew she'd been looking at me. Her facial expression when I removed my cover-up confirmed that my suspicion was correct. I didn't think Lowe was aware that her reaction was so obvious and hoped she couldn't see my response to the attention. The water cooled my skin but did nothing to tamp down the heat inside me as I tried to focus on the beautiful underwater landscape in front of me. One of the gentlemen aboard had assisted Shirley down the steps and said he would swim with her. That was one less thing for me to worry about. I had a hard-enough time remembering to breathe through my mouth and not inhale any seawater.

The water was so clear the blues and greens on the reef popped with color. Schools of fish the size of footballs with bright-yellow vertical stripes swam around me. I shook my head in disgust as two men in dark swim trunks tried to grab several of them as they swam by. Either they hadn't listened to Captain Nate, or more than likely, these two clowns thought the rules didn't apply to them. Movement to my right drew my attention from the men, and I spotted Lowe swimming down toward the reef. I hoped she respected the fragile nature of the coral, and as I floated on the surface, I was relieved when she stopped several feet from the delicate ecoscape. She moved her arms and legs to stay in place for a few moments before righting herself and heading back toward the surface.

I couldn't take my eyes off Lowe as she swam, fluid and graceful in the clear water. Her legs were long, with much more exposed today than I'd seen so far.

I hadn't slept much last night, my dreams centered around Lowe and what would have happened if I'd allowed our kiss to continue. It was bad enough that I looked for her everywhere I went on the ship. I couldn't control that urge any more than I could control my dreams, especially when they centered on a certain tall, striking blonde.

I was hoping that the bottle and a half of wine I'd shared with Raul last night after leaving the party would have made me semi-comatose and I'd sleep through the night. But it had failed to dampen the steamy eroticism of my subconscious. My dream last night had started with Lowe not walking away.

*Lowe had pulled me close, and I was powerless to keep from stepping into her embrace. The heat from her body enveloped me, and I succumbed to the temptation of her kisses. Lowe's mouth was soft and tentative and increased its demand as I eagerly kissed her back. Needing to feel her body against me, I wrapped my arms around her neck and rose onto my toes.*

*Lowe's hands were hot against my skin, and I pulled her starched shirt from her pants. I needed to touch her, feel her, taste her. Not able to wait, I lifted her shirt higher and kissed the exposed skin. She moaned and inhaled sharply, and I soared with the knowledge that I was pleasing her. I needed more and tugged at the buttons, my hands trembling so much that Lowe pushed them away and unbuttoned a few herself.*

*I pushed her undershirt above her breasts and stared in awe. Lowe had the most magnificent breasts, full of desire, her erect nipples begging to be licked.*

Unfortunately, I was so caught up in reliving my dream, I wasn't paying attention to the position of my snorkel, and it dropped below the water line. The end contained a lightweight ball similar to a fishing bobber that, when submerged, floated to the top and blocked water from entering. As a result, I didn't inhale seawater. However, I also wasn't able to inhale any oxygen. I fought a moment of panic before realizing what I'd done and lifted the end of my snorkel out of the water.

For the remainder of the forty minutes we were in the water, I was acutely aware of Lowe's location and often found her swimming nearby. After another bout of sucking dead air, I realized I needed to get out of the water before I got a lungful.

I swam a short distance to the beach of the nearby island. Captain Nate had said we were moored an easy swim from Daydream Island, less than a mile long and half as wide. Bethany had told Lowe that we were allowed to explore the island, and it was more than apparent she wanted to explore Lowe.

I pulled my fins off just before my feet hit the soft, powdery white sand of the beach, and the tide gently pushed me the rest of the way in. I left the fins, along with my snorkel and mask, next to a large outcropping of rocks about fifty feet in from the shore. Unless the high tide rolled in very quickly, they'd be there when I returned.

I wasn't going far, planning to just walk down the beach to clear my head. I had about thirty minutes before I had to be back on the boat for my SNUBA session. A five-minute walk in one direction, then back, and another five to get my gear on and swim back to the boat left me plenty of time.

The island was beautiful. Colorful tropical fish swam lazily in the crystal-clear water in the bay. The inland rain forest was thick and green, highlighted by the sound of birds squawking in the trees. A small, private resort was supposed to be nestled on this tiny island, but I saw no sign of anyone else. I had the beach to myself.

The water lapped at my feet as I strolled along the shoreline. The push and pull of the waves reminded me of my feelings toward Lowe. The pull of attraction was undeniable, and if I wasn't very, very careful, I'd be swept away by a force as fast and as dangerous as a rip current. I wouldn't be able to do anything to stop the strong, narrow tide of desire from pulling me into her. I was exhausted from trying to swim directly away from the overwhelming attraction between us.

I walked for another few minutes before turning to go back to my gear, and when I did, I saw a familiar figure walking toward me. My heart raced, and my pulse skyrocketed.

We met under a large tree, its canopy shielding us from the summer sun. Lowe's skin was tan from our outdoor activities, her suit wet. Like me, she had evidently stored her gear somewhere on the deserted beach.

Smoldering blue eyes caught and held mine. The flame of desire burning brightly took my breath away. An overwhelming awareness, an insistent throb of desire I had never experienced coursed through me. I flushed as Lowe searched my eyes for the answer she was looking for. I had no idea if she'd find it because I didn't even know if I knew.

Lowe reached out and brushed my cheek. Her fingers branded my skin, and I wanted her mark over my entire body. My mind went numb, and all sense, common or otherwise, left me. She looked uncertain, doubt creeping into her strong, confident bearing. I wanted to scream kiss me, but I said nothing. I wanted to touch her bare skin but didn't move. I wanted to step into her arms and never let go but stood still.

It was obviously my move, and when I didn't make it, Lowe dropped her hand, turned, and walked away.

I don't know if I was relieved or disappointed. On the one hand, I'd been insistent we didn't cross the line, yet the chemistry and attraction between us was off the charts. This was the perfect setting to consummate a forbidden encounter. With a few steps we'd have complete privacy to release pent-up desire that was as combustible as dry tinder on a hot, summer day.

With each step that took Lowe farther away from me, I wanted to scream at the idiotic rules that governed me. Justifications of my actions if I were to call her back raced through my head. Anyone else in this situation probably wouldn't have hesitated. My integrity, no, my fear of just how fast and far I'd fallen for her kept me from saying anything. As she disappeared, I'd never felt so alone.

Back on board, I drank from a bottle of water, letting the warm sun dry me. I slipped my sunglasses on and waited for Lowe to return to the boat. If Lowe could watch me go into the water, I had the right to watch her come out.

Lowe ascended the ladder, and when she stepped onto the deck, I didn't know if I'd been rewarded for my diligence or would be cursed again tonight by the striking image of water sliding down her fabulous body.

We ate a light snack, and then it was our turn to SNUBA. Our rights relinquished by our signatures on the bottom of the forms, we donned wet suits, and after a ten-minute orientation we were in the water.

Lowe was paired with another rookie, who, after a long look at her, introduced herself in a ridiculously sultry voice and asked Lowe to keep an eye on her. Anne put me with another experienced diver, a large woman who chatted to herself the entire time we were getting ready.

I was relieved that Lowe would be on another line. Her constant scrutiny, though flattering, kept me in a continuous state of arousal. I was exhausted from deflecting her innuendos. I had absolutely no doubt of what she'd rather be doing, and as much as I pushed back, I wanted to give in.

Doing the right thing was exhausting, and if we had met before she boarded in Sydney or a week from now, things would be different, very different. As it was, I'd spent almost every moment since I ran into her that first day trying to figure a way out of this predicament and into her arms.

The heat from her eyes on my ass when we were on the stairs turned my legs to Jell-O, and I could barely put one foot on each step. I wanted to toss "Hi, my name is Bethany and I'm here to make sure you have a good time" overboard. Jealousy is not attractive, especially when it was uncalled for. But it was there nonetheless.

Anne swam by, and I gave her a thumbs-up after she signaled the amount of time remaining on our dive. I found Lowe about thirty yards away. The crystal-clear water accentuated the smooth movements of her long arms and legs. She looked perfectly comfortable as she explored her surroundings.

Over the last two weeks it was apparent that Lowe was an unusual woman. She was self-assured, smart without being a know-it-all, and the best-looking woman I'd seen in a long time—if ever. I wasn't drawn to any one thing, like the color of her eyes or the way her left cheek dimpled when she smiled. She could have been arrogant and stuck-up like her parents, but she wasn't. Not at all. She was her own self-reliant woman, or at least she appeared to be.

I'd thrown caution out the porthole, and against my better judgment and even though I knew it was wrong, I finally admitted I'd fallen for Lowe Carter.

The thought overwhelmed me, and I forgot how to breathe, at least through my regulator. I swallowed a few mouthfuls of the Coral Sea, the salty water somehow infiltrating my mask and making my eyes burn. Anne was quickly beside me, concern apparent behind her face mask.

I put the heel of my hand on my mask between my eyes and pushed, blowing out through my nose. My mask cleared instantly, and I gave Anne another thumbs-up. She watched me for a few moments longer before kicking her fins and swimming away.

I looked around for Lowe again, the woman I'd almost drowned over, and found her watching me. She gave me the "are you okay?" signal, and I indicated I was. I think if I'd said otherwise, she'd have tossed her gear off and rescued me. That was a nice thought.

All too soon, Anne gave us the sign to head to the surface. Lowe and her tether-partner surfaced first, followed by two others, and then it was my turn.

Back on the boat, Lowe handed me a towel.

"That was awesome," she said, her expression reflecting her comment. Her eyes sparkled, and my stomach did a summersault. I couldn't remember the last time it had flip-flopped like that. Oh yeah, the last time Lowe looked at me.

"It is, isn't it? Most people say that their first time." OMG, that actually came out of my mouth. I gasped and felt the heat of embarrassment creep up my neck, while heat of another kind shot in the opposite direction.

"Yes, I suppose it's true," she said simply, not reacting to my own provocative statement. Thank God, because her look was hot, and I had no strength to resist, and no will to.

Anne helped me out of my gear while Bethany had her hands on Lowe in more places than the buckles.

"I've got this, thanks," Lowe said, stepping away from her with an exasperated expression.

Lowe grabbed a towel from the stack and wiped her face. Then she rubbed it through her hair, which stuck out at all angles in a cute, disheveled way.

Back on the top deck, I reached into my bag and pulled out my sunscreen. I tried to ignore Lowe watching me as I rubbed the thick lotion on my legs and arms.

"Need some on your back?"

I should have said no. I should have put my tank top back on. I should have stayed back on the *Escape*.

"Thanks. I appreciate it."

Lowe's hands on me felt wonderful. They were strong and smooth as she spread the sunscreen over my skin. Somewhere along the way, they shifted from medicinal to sensual, and my body sprang to life. My pulse throbbed between my legs, and my heart beat so fast it sounded like the rat-a-tat of a snare drum. My head fell forward when Lowe rubbed my neck, the tense muscles relaxed under the skillful hands. I grabbed the rail and locked my elbows to support my suddenly weak knees. I felt Lowe's warm breath on my neck when she stepped behind me. A shiver ran through me, and she had to have noticed.

"Cold?"

Not hardly, I thought, but only shook my head. A giggle and the pop of the top of a can reminded me we weren't alone on the deck. I wished we were so Lowe could continue to have her hands on me, but in many other places.

"There, that should do it."

Lowe's voice was husky, her hand shaking when she gave me the tube of sunscreen. I was glad to see I wasn't the only one affected by the last few minutes. Bethany hovered nearby like a pesky drone, but Lowe ignored her.

An hour later we had docked and were waiting for the crowd to disembark when Lowe asked, "Can I interest you in a cup of coffee before we head back to the ship?"

"What is it with you Americans and coffee?" I asked, teasing.

"I think it's a euphemism for do you want to get together?" Lowe looked a little sheepish.

"Is that what *you* mean?" I was tired of dancing around this— whatever this was. Lowe looked shocked at my question but then relieved.

"What do you think?"

Way to throw it back into my court, Lowe, I thought, but then decided to stop thinking.

"I know I don't have to be back on board until nine tomorrow morning," I said bravely. "I know there's a hotel not far from here.

And I know if I don't feel your hands and mouth on me in the next ten minutes, I might self-combust."

There, I'd said it. I'd jumped without a blindfold and with both feet into what I knew would be an abyss of carnal pleasure—and possibly unemployment.

I must have caught Lowe off guard because she didn't say anything for a few moments, nor did she move or give any other indication she was up for this. I hadn't read this situation wrong, or at least I hoped I hadn't. The longer Lowe didn't reply, the more afraid I became. Finally, after what felt like an eternity, she leaned near and kissed me.

"How do you like your morning coffee?"

## CHAPTER TWENTY-THREE

We strolled down the street more casually than I wanted to. I'd have run the distance in record time if Lowe had given any indication she wanted to. We walked a block, turned left, and half a block later entered the lobby of a small, boutique hotel.

I reached into my bag to pull out my wallet as we approached the registration desk, but Lowe put her hand on my arm. Words weren't necessary. I didn't have much money in my account, but I would have mortgaged my future to be alone and naked with her.

Lowe's hand shook as she scribbled her name on the register. She wasn't as calm as she appeared to be, which thrilled me. Jesus, Faith, stop philosophizing and just go with it, I told myself right before Lowe turned toward me, a bright-green key card in her hand. Talk about a beacon of what was to come.

Lowe kept her hand on the small of my back as we walked across the small lobby. It was a nice touch. A connection, rather than possession.

The elevator crawled to the third floor, and I grew more nervous as each second passed. I had no reason to be; I'd done this hundreds of times. Okay, maybe not exactly this, and I have no idea how many times I'd had sex, but it was nerve-racking being with a new person, and even more so with Lowe.

The first time is usually a little awkward and clumsy, arms and legs bumping into each other. Elbows connecting with teeth, hair in the wrong places, feet getting stuck in pants. Am I too loud or not vocal enough, too fast or too slow? One finger or two? Three or more? Ouch. What if I come too fast or not fast enough? What if I can't come at all? Do I fake it or try something new? The stress involved with having sex is so astronomical, sometimes I'm surprised anyone does it at all.

The elevator doors opened, and my mind continued to ramble as we walked down the hall. The click of the lock on the door echoed in the empty hall. Or was it just in my head?

Lowe held the door open for me to enter first, her actions more than mere politeness. She was giving me a chance to change my mind. I had no doubt I could please Lowe, make her quiver with desire, lose herself in sensation. How did I know this? Because I'd seen the desire in her eyes, the way she flushed when I looked at her, the way her hand shook a few moments ago. She wanted me as much as I wanted her. I didn't hesitate to cross the threshold.

How I didn't grab Faith and pull her into one of the many alleys we passed is beyond me. I had never wanted someone as bad as I wanted Faith. It wasn't just her physical beauty but what was inside that made me crazy for her. And when she'd said she needed my mouth on her, my vision had blurred, and my head spun.

There's just something sexy about a woman taking ownership of what she wants and needs. When she takes off her own clothes because she wants to be touched. When she calls for the check because she wants to be naked and alone with you. The way she enters the room knowing full well what's going to happen once we close and lock the door. Somehow, I kept my composure and managed to act like an adult and check us in and get this far.

When the door closed behind me, I was uncharacteristically unsure what to do next. Did we strip or take each other's clothes off? Did we sit and make small talk? Order some wine? Chastely pull the covers back and climb in?

I didn't need to worry, because Faith turned and pushed me against the door, her kisses impatient. Momentarily stunned, I quickly gathered my wits and kissed her back. Actually, I did more than kiss her. I tugged her shirt up and slid my hands over her warm, smooth back. Faith moved closer and melted against me.

Our bodies fit together like they were made specifically for each other. Two women making love was the most erotic thing I can ever imagine. Curves molded into valleys, hard met soft, and knowing where to touch was a sixth sense.

Faith's mouth was hot, her hands insistent, her body tense. Our tongues fought for control while our hands tangled in straps and spandex. Finally, our suits lay on the floor, and she groaned when I touched her.

Faith pressed her knee between my legs, and it was my turn to sigh in pleasure. I ground my crotch into the hard thigh, and my head started to spin. I felt fabulous, like I was slipping from reality into perfect pleasure. Stars blinked in front of me, and I knew I was going to come. I wanted to wait, to feel Faith's fingers on me, in me, but my overwhelming desire refused to listen. My orgasm roared in my ears and rolled over me like a thundercloud exploding overhead. I pulled Faith closer. I wanted to be in her, and lights flashed, drums pounded as my climax took me to another place, another realm that was perfect yet frightening.

I was floating back to reality, and when my head hit the pillow, I knew this was no dream. Faith's body warmed me, the heat comforting and exhilarating. Lips replaced hands, fingers searched, explored, and took ownership. Faith demanded my body, and I readily, eagerly complied. Warm breath on cool wetness did nothing to quench the burning desire at my center. Faith knew just what to do, and her lips and tongue brought me to orgasm once again. I stifled a scream, my breathing rapid. Within the earthly confines of the bed, I soared.

I thought I was dreaming and prayed I wouldn't wake up. Faith was hovering above me gazing at me, her eyes filled with desire. The heat of her body on top of mine radiated through me. My hands held her hair back from her face, and I could easily pull her lips to mine. But I didn't. This was no dream. This was her show, she was in charge, and I was more than willing to give her free rein, for now.

She started at the base of my ear, covering my jaw with light kisses. Her breasts pressed against mine, her nipples hard. I don't know what had led up to us being here, and I didn't care. All I wanted was for her to not stop the magical things she was doing to me.

Her lips roamed over my neck and I tilted my head back, so she could go wherever she wanted. She shifted, and I had a moment of panic when I thought she was leaving but calmed when she simply moved lower.

Faith's hot, wet mouth circled first one breast, then the other, tormenting me. I wanted her lips on my nipple, sucking and nipping almost to the point of making me come. Faith either read my mind or I begged, because that was exactly what she did next.

I tried to be still but gave up. What was the point? I was enjoying everything she was doing to me, so why not let her know? If I did, she wouldn't stop. At least I hoped so.

I arched up when she sucked hard on my left nipple, and I think I called her name. My knees came up, and I felt her warm, wet center against my thigh. Faith moaned with the contact. Cool air hit my wet nipples as Faith moved lower.

"Jesus, that feels good." I fought not to squirm as Faith kissed and caressed my stomach. The disparity in our heights made no difference as she moved even lower, her shoulders separating my legs. I let my knees fall open, giving her complete access to all of me. This wasn't the time to be shy, which I'm not. It was time to feel and experience all Faith was willing to give. And she knew exactly what to do.

She kissed that soft spot where my lips meet my inner thigh, then ran her tongue over the path of her kisses. She explored me with soft, trembling fingers and eyes filled with hunger.

I was in agony and ecstasy at the same time. I didn't want her to stop, but I needed her to touch me, kiss me, lick me. My hips rose instinctively anytime her mouth got close. Finally, she granted my wish, my desire, my need, and she swiped her tongue over my clit.

She had me so wound up I had to clench my jaw and ball my fists not to come. I needed release, my body begging for it, but I knew Faith wasn't done, and I wanted this to go on forever. Stroke after agonizing stroke, Faith expertly took me higher and higher until I was dizzy with need. I moved toward a bright light in the distance until it exploded in front of me. I cried out, my hips bucking in orgasm. I grabbed Faith's head and ground my clit into her. My climax was so powerful, I felt like I was coming out of my skin. Out of control, I rode wave after wave of pleasure until I lay spent and breathless on the sheet.

Gasping to breathe, I felt Faith straddle my leg and rock against me. Her clit was hard and her breasts within reach. I raised up and pulled a tight nipple into my mouth. Faith moaned again and pushed harder against me.

She tangled her fingers in my hair as she held my mouth against her breast. Her pace quickened, and mine mirrored hers. The idea of a woman pleasuring herself makes me crazy, and in an instant, I was ready to come again.

Faith rode my leg like it was the last orgasm of her life, and I let her. She called my name several times and begged me not to stop. I had no problem giving her exactly what she needed.

The ringing of a cell phone woke me. It was still dark, and I rolled over to reach for it, thinking it was one of my managers. I bumped against a warm body and immediately remembered where I was and who was answering the phone beside me.

"Hello."

Faith's voice was just above a whisper. I looked over her shoulder to the digital clock on the table. Less than an hour since she fell asleep in my arms. A little more than twelve hours since we closed the hotel room door behind us. Between then and now we'd made love at least a dozen times, with countless orgasms between us. God, I loved being a woman and making love with a woman. Orgasms could be endless. We'd ordered room service somewhere around eight last night, and now it was almost six. I snuggled behind her.

"No. I'm not on till nine."

I heard a male voice on the other end of the conversation but couldn't make out what he was saying. It wasn't any of my business anyway.

"No, François. I can't. "

Faith listened, her body stiffening and tense.

"I made plans."

Did those plans include this?

"I'm sorry, François. It's really none of your business with whom or where. I'll be at work at nine like the schedule shows."

Someone on the *Escape* was obviously hassling Faith. I wanted to take the phone from her and tell this jerk to leave her alone.

"You can't do that, François." Faith sat up, the covers spilling off her and pooling on the bed around her waist. The bathroom light was on, casting a soft warm glow into the predawn room.

"If you changed the schedule after I left the ship and didn't notify me, you can't expect me to know that."

Faith's voice was angry, a tone I'd never heard before.

"Don't do it, François. No, I'm not threatening you. I'm trying to save you from embarrassment if this goes to the area supervisor or Captain Waverly."

More talking was coming from Faith's caller, the voice raised and abrupt. Faith, though not happy, remained calm and professional.

"No, François, it's not that I won't. I can't. Even if I could, I'm at least an hour away."

I sat up, pulling the pillows against the headboard behind my back. I tugged the sheet up over my breasts, not because I was suddenly shy, but because the room was cool. Sometime during the evening we'd turned the thermostat down, our bodies hot with passion.

"Yes, François. That's my final answer. I'll see you at nine. Good-bye."

Faith punched the red button on her phone and let her head drop, her shoulders slumping.

"I take it everything is not okay?" No shit, Sherlock, I thought. That's pretty obvious. It took several moments before Faith replied.

"No, but it will be."

"Anything I can do?"

Faith looked over her shoulder at me. Her hair was mussed, fatigue in her eyes. She had that just-fucked look about her, and, feeling like a cad, I wanted to do it again.

"Or did I already do it?" I asked, addressing the elephant in the room. Faith continued to study me. I wished I could read her mind.

"No, nothing you can do, and you didn't do anything," she said, sounding defeated. She got out of bed and headed toward the bathroom.

I heard the water run for a few minutes before the door opened and she walked toward me. I was surprised she was still naked. I had expected her to have on one of the white, fluffy robes hanging behind the door.

Faith stopped at the foot of the bed. She was beautiful, exquisite, standing in front of me completely comfortable. I kept my eyes on hers, even though I wanted to pull her back into bed. This wasn't the time.

"I take that back," she said, her voice strong. "You did do something."

My heart leapt into my throat. Yep, here it comes. The rebuke, the chastisement, the blame.

"You made me feel wonderful. You did exactly what I asked you to." She blushed a becoming shade of pink. "And more than a few things I didn't. I have," she looked at the clock, "two hours and twenty-five minutes until I have to be back. And I want you to do it to me all over again."

Who was I to say no?

## CHAPTER TWENTY-FOUR

I didn't want to think about what was going to happen when we got back on the ship. No one could know that Lowe and I had spent the night together, certainly not yesterday afternoon and this morning until thirty minutes ago, exploring everything two people could do to each other. I'm sure we left a few things out but...

"Would you like to stop for some breakfast?" Lowe asked.

We were getting close to the ship, passing several cafés and small bistros.

I wasn't hungry, my stomach in knots about what was sure to be a confrontation with François. Pulling myself together was the first on my to-do list, followed by putting on my game face for work. If François pushed his position that I was AWOL for my early a.m. shift, I'd request the supervisor pull the e-records of the schedule changes. I'm all for personal accountability, but I'd checked the schedule right before I disembarked. It was no different than it had been for the past three days. I had an impeccable record, and his power play was not going to blemish it. I wasn't ready to think where my dalliance with Lowe fit in. What is it they say, no blood, no foul? It's not against the law if you don't get caught? That was just an excuse for bad behavior, and I'd have to deal with the consequences when they came up.

"No," I said, probably too sharply. "I have to get back." Seeing my way out of an awkward situation, I said, "But you go ahead. I have to check in and get ready for work."

I picked up my pace and tried hard not to run to the gangplank of the *Escape*. I knew Lowe must be confused at my complete one-eighty-degree turn-about. For the past eighteen hours I'd been on her, under her, and inside her. Now I was practically pretending those hours didn't exist and we were again almost strangers. How fucked up was that?

I waved my badge across the reader at the base of the walkway. Not only did I receive a green light indicating I was authorized to board, but I also had to deal with the knowing look of Raul, who was on duty at that station.

"Don't say it," I said, putting my hand up.

"I don't have to. That red mark on your neck says it all."

My legs froze, and I wrapped both hands around my neck. Holy Christ. If I had a hickey, François would blow a French gasket.

Raul burst out laughing. "Busted," he said, almost doubling over, he was laughing so hard.

"You bastard," I said, more relieved than angry. He was my ship BFF after all.

"François is looking for you." He'd stopped laughing and was suddenly serious.

"I know. I need a shower before I deal with him." I'd had one before we left the hotel, but Lowe had joined me, and we'd used every drop of hot water. I needed to wash away any residual traces of the woman who had taken control of my body and my mind. No. That wasn't right. I'd willingly given her my body, and my mind was lost on my own.

"Well, he's prowling around the deck, so I suggest you take the back stairs."

"Thanks. I owe you." I kissed him on his scratchy cheek.

"The only thing you owe me is the complete details over a bottle of beer."

"It'll take at least a case," I said over my shoulder, and Raul's whistle followed me to the stairs.

❖

What in the hell just happened, I thought as Faith left me standing alone in the middle of the sidewalk. After the most mind-blowing, sexually satisfying night of my life, I'd been…what…cast off like a one-night stand?

I could handle that if that's what it was, but I certainly thought it was more than that. I thought Faith had believed so as well. Obviously, she was in some kind of hot water with that François guy on the phone. Maybe she didn't want him seeing us together, which might aggravate the situation even more. I'd have to ask her about it later, but my gut told me I might have a hard time even finding her.

My stomach growled, and I took Faith up on her suggestion that I have breakfast. We didn't depart until two this afternoon, so I had plenty of time to sit and enjoy the warm sunshine.

A very attractive waitress took my order and winked at me before moving on to the next table. Did every woman in this country get an email to hit on me? Not that I minded, but where were they on my last trip?

For the next hour I drank several cups of coffee and nibbled on my breakfast. It was tasty, but every time I thought of Faith, which was practically the entire time, my stomach tingled. And when images of her as we made love flashed in my brain, I completely lost my appetite for food.

Faith had been insatiable. Actually, we both were, our coupling fast, almost furious, then slow and languid. We laughed, giggled like schoolgirls, whispered each other's names, and begged for release. We talked about everything and nothing and, most of the time, didn't say anything at all, our bodies speaking for us.

One particular time Faith had straddled me, her warm, wet center pressed against my stomach. Slowly she rocked against me, her eyes closed. I reached for her, but she brushed my hands away, using her own to tweak her nipples. Clearly I was to be an observer. Her head dropped back, exposing her long neck, her long hair caressing my thighs like a feather.

My heart pounded at the sheer beauty of Faith pleasuring herself. Faster and faster she rocked, pinching her nipples hard. Her breathing became rapid and shallow, a light sheen of sweat covering her. She was glorious, all woman, and she took herself over the edge. Just watching Faith climax was a breathtaking sight I would never forget, and, surprisingly, I came with her.

As she had settled down from her climax, she leaned forward, her hands on either side of my shoulders. Her hair shrouded out the world, and I wanted to stay that way forever. The realization pulled all the air from my lungs, and I'd pushed it aside until now, sitting at a small table in the bustling tourist shopping area.

What was I supposed to do now? I'd never been in this position. I'd had some medium-term relationships with women, but none that included seeing my future with them. They were professional and interesting, with complete lives of their own. Maybe they didn't need me that much, and obviously I hadn't needed them.

Faith, however, was different. She was the complete opposite of the women in my past, which was more than a little scary. What would I do with her? What did we have in common? I knew very little about her, her irritating quirks or political views. Not that those would be showstoppers, but they were important. The most important challenge was that I was completely in over my head. Way over.

Maybe my mother was right, God forbid. This couldn't go anywhere. I live in Phoenix with a company to run. Faith lives on a ship, for God's sake. This is where her job is. She wouldn't leave it behind for me, and I wouldn't ask her to. Good God, we've only known each other for not even three weeks.

I was going home in a few days. Or at least I was planning to. I had a return flight out of Sydney when we returned. Maybe if I stayed a few more days I'd get her out of my system. Or maybe something would come up that changed my mind. Maybe I'd grow tired of her. I had a better chance of getting hit by lightning in this cloudless sky, I realized. I toyed with the idea of not returning to the ship and catching a flight back to the States but then dumped it just as quickly. It would be ghastly expensive, and I didn't want to have to deal with my mother for the rest of my life.

I looked for Faith as I boarded. It was after eleven, and, based on her phone conversation, I knew she was working. I looked in the two restaurants on the main deck and the shops in the corridor on my way to the stairs to my parents' deck. I wasn't expecting to see her, but a girl could hope.

My mother and Victoria were sitting in the living room when I closed the door behind me.

"Lowe?"

Shit. I'd tried to be quiet so I didn't face an inquisition, but my luck was consistent, to say the least.

"Yes?" I didn't move any farther into the apartment, hoping I could slip into my suite quietly.

"Would you come here, please? I refuse to yell across the room." My mother never raised her voice. I entered the large room and braced for the worst.

"Are you just getting in?"

I could not believe that, even at thirty-six years old, I could let my mother still make me feel like a guilty teenager sneaking in after curfew.

"Do you need something?" I asked instead of answering her question. She knew damn good and well I had. I was certain Victoria had gloated over the fact every hour on the hour when I didn't show for breakfast.

"I'd like to know where you were last night. We expected you for dinner." Her tone was harsh, and Victoria wore a self-satisfied smirk.

I was keyed up and tired and not in the mood for this. "Do you really want to know where I was, Mother?" Two could play at this game. If she wanted to know, she'd get it.

"Yes, tell us, Lowe." My sister joined in. "Where were you all night?"

I ignored her and waited for my mother to answer my question.

"A little common courtesy is not too much to ask, Lowe. We had no idea where you were and were worried."

Nosey was more like it. "I'm sorry, Mother. I should have called. I guess I'm just used to not having to report in. Do you need anything else?"

My mother stared at me, her eyes boring into me as they had so effectively when I was a child. I was always able to keep my mouth shut, but Victoria, on the other hand, always sang like the proverbial canary, always pointing at me.

"Is that all you have to say? I should have called?" Victoria asked. Some things never change.

"To Mother, yes. If you have something else you want to talk about, Victoria, we don't need to bother Mother with it."

I turned and headed down the hall to my suite, knowing Victoria would follow. I didn't say anything until we were in my room, the door closed.

"What is it, Victoria?" I was in no mood for her sanctimonious shit.

"Where were you? Mother was worried. She—"

"She was not. I'm a grown woman and can take care of myself. You…" I pointed my finger at her. "You seem to be pretty interested in where I was. You keep telling me I need to share more about my life, so if you really want to know, I was making love with a beautiful woman. We spent the afternoon, evening, all night, and this morning together in a hotel. The only time we got out of bed was to get a glass of water or order room service. Anything else you want to know? I don't kiss and tell, so don't expect any details."

Victoria paled, then grew red. She'd asked for it.

"Was it that crew member?" she practically snarled.

"Not that it's any of your fucking business, but no." No way was I going to bring Faith into this.

"How do you do that? Sleep with someone you just met?"

"Let me assure you, Victoria, that very little sleep was involved."

"That's disgusting," she spat, her face mirroring her words.

"You may think so, but the lady had absolutely no complaints. Now if you don't mind, I need a shower and a nap, obviously."

"You're nothing more than—"

"Than what, Victoria? Honest about who I am?" My sister didn't know what to say, so I ended the conversation. "You can show yourself out." I calmly shut the bathroom door behind me.

From the privacy of my bathroom I stripped and took a good look at myself in the mirror. It had been several hours since I was with Faith, but my body still hummed from recent great sex. My skin glowed, my breasts still full from arousal. My nipples were sore, but in a good way. A very good way.

I let the water cascade over me, its warmth soothing my tired muscles. I washed my hair and slathered shower gel over my arms and legs. When I reached my woman parts, I couldn't help but remember the feel of Faith's skillful hands making me come almost in record time earlier this morning.

*I'd let her shower first, but when I imagined her naked, I couldn't lie in bed alone. The shower doors were clear, giving me an excellent view of her perfect backside. I watched like a voyeur for as long as I could stand it before I knocked on the door.*

*Faith yelped. "Shit, you scared me." She wiped the water off her face and pushed her hair back.*

*"May I join you?" God, please say yes, I prayed. My prayers were answered when she opened the door a crack.*

*"I have to get to work."*

*"Okay."*

*"No funny business."*

*There was nothing funny about what I wanted to do to her. "I promise, no funny business." I crossed my heart, and Faith watched, her eyes focused on my breasts. I saw the vein in her neck pulse faster. I knew that sign, and I stepped inside.*

I closed my eyes and brought myself to orgasm, imagining Faith's fingers on me. I finished my shower, slipped into boxers and a T-shirt, and fell into bed.

## CHAPTER TWENTY-FIVE

F rançois made my day a living hell. The schedule had me in the gym for my entire shift, but an hour after I relieved Joanne, he moved me to the kitchen, then to a different post every hour. I wouldn't have minded the variety, but the positions were the busiest ones on the ship. I was exhausted both physically and mentally, but I'd be damned if he would know that.

The third time I showed up in the laundry, the supervisor asked me whose shit list I'd gotten on. I just smiled and made some benign, safe comment and got to work. François was my shadow, and if he wasn't looking over my shoulder, he was watching me from across the room. I'm surprised I didn't see his feet in the bathroom stall next to me. Not only did I have him nipping at my heels, but I was also on heightened alert for any sighting of Lowe. That was the last thing I needed today. The only good thing was that François made no reference to his phone call this morning, nor was there any indication he was going to write me up. If he couldn't get to me that way, he tried the other.

I punched out at 6:45 and was on my way to my room to collapse when I ran into Raul by the payroll office.

"Chica, you owe me a story and twelve beers," he said, much too happily.

"No. I owe you a story over twelve beers consumed by you and me." I emphasized the joint-drinking part. "But not tonight, Raul. I'm exhausted, and François ran my ass off today."

"He has it in for you, chica."

"Tell me something I don't know," I said as we walked down the narrow corridor. Whether it was because I was a lesbian, a hard worker, a female, or some other stupid reason, I'd concluded that François had stayed up all night thinking of ways he could make me miserable. He was always just this side of harassment, so I couldn't do much other than complete my job the best I could. Thankfully, I didn't have to work with him very often.

"You do not look well. You need nourishment."

Raul could be somebody's grandmother, the way he dotes on people and is completely convinced that food is the solution to everything that ails anyone.

"I'm too tired to eat. I'm going to bed and not wake up until my shift tomorrow."

"What time are you on?"

"Two till eleven. I'm scheduled for Remington's. But who knows? I do know, though, if I don't lie down and get some sleep, I'll fall down."

"She was that good, huh?" Raul asked, raising and lowering his eyebrows à la Groucho Marx.

"Better." I hip-bumped him.

"I'll keep an eye out for your señorita."

"What?"

"Lowe Carter. If I see her, I'll bring her down."

"No."

"No?"

"No. She is not my señorita, and I do not want you to bring her to my cabin." I stopped and laid my arm on his, turning him to face me. "I mean it, Raul. Do not do it." Raul was a romantic and wanted everyone to be in love.

"Did you not have a good time with her?"

Several other staff passed us, and I waited until they were out of earshot to answer.

"I do not want to talk about Lowe Carter, and I do not want her anywhere near my cabin. Understand?"

"I understand," he said quietly.

"I mean it, Raul." I warned him again. "You know the rules."

"Okay. I will let you rest," he said, clearly dejected. "But tomorrow is another day."

For sure it would be, and I hoped it would be better than this one.

After a hot shower, I crawled under the covers, pulling the sheet up to my chin. I started to think about Lowe, but I forced myself to think of something else. That lasted about three minutes.

I dreamed about warm skin and soft kisses. A touch that ignited my core and smoldering blue eyes that caught and held mine. Lips that were so close we shared the same air. Sighs of pleasure, moans of ecstasy, and shouts of release filling the space around us. Being blatantly erotic and bashfully shy. Sharing everything and holding nothing back, and completely losing my mind.

# CHAPTER TWENTY-SIX

*Day Eighteen*
*At sea*
*Great Barrier Reef to Sydney*

I woke horny as hell and not that much more rested than when I lay down. I'd tossed and turned all night, fully expecting Raul to knock on my door with Lowe in hand. My breasts were swollen with desire, my clit pounding for relief, my breath coming in gasps. My hand was already between my legs, the other pinching my nipple. I ignored the ringing of my alarm clock, and it wasn't long until I climaxed.

"Holy fuck," I said after I was finally able to catch my breath. That was the most powerful self-induced orgasm in my life, and I struggled to focus. For a moment I expected Lowe to slide up my body and kiss me, my scent on her lips; the dream was that real.

I stared at the ceiling, watching the fan cast shadows in the early morning sun. I needed to get up, pull myself together, and get to work. As much as I wanted to, I couldn't lie in bed all day fantasizing about Lowe. I swung my legs over the side and stood.

A wave of dizziness swam over me, and I grabbed the headboard until it passed. I was probably dehydrated, and I hadn't eaten much in the last forty-eight hours. Raul was right. I did need to take better care of myself.

After a long, hot shower and two bottles of water, I closed and locked the door behind me. My head was still a little foggy, but I'd have some coffee and push through the inconvenience.

I couldn't help but look for Lowe as I approached The Cuppa. It was busy, several people waiting for their order with another five or six in line. I looked at my watch. I had time, so I stepped behind one of the residents.

"Monica, you need to get this order to the Carters on fifteen," a man wearing a white chef hat said from his place behind the counter.

I knew the order was for Lowe's parents. A rush of warmth flowed through me at the thought of her. I closed my eyes to banish the image of Lowe lying naked on the large hotel bed, her back arched as she came. I opened them quickly—not a good idea. If I kept this up, I'd probably drop somebody's meal or hot coffee in their lap.

I switched topics and thought about my mum and Angelica. My watch had two faces, one set to local time, whatever that was, and the other on Florida time. It was after dinner, and my mum had probably cleaned up the kitchen and was helping Angelica with her homework.

I stepped out of line and reached for my phone. It had been a week since I'd talked to my mum, and I'd never gone this long without calling. She never called me because she never knew where exactly I was. Ship-to-shore calls were free for the crew but ghastly expensive the other way around. She had the emergency number, but she'd never had to use it.

At fifty-two, my mum has had a hard life. We immigrated to Florida when I was ten, and my mum found her new country challenging. She fell for the wrong guy, and by the time she met the right one, I was fourteen years old. The man I called Pop had moved us to Tampa but died in a roofing accident shortly thereafter, leaving behind my mother and my unborn baby sister Angelica.

My mum has psoriatic arthritis, an autoimmune disorder that affects her joints, primarily her wrists, hands, and knees. Getting out of bed in the morning can sometimes be a challenge for Mum, but she pushes through the pain and lethargy to get Angelica to school and herself to work. When Angelica was four, she was diagnosed as being on the autism spectrum, which meant they slapped a defining label on her. If not for the diligent work of my mum, Angelica would have languished in elementary school until she aged out. The money I send home every month pays Angelica's tuition in a special school and for one-on-one specialized therapy.

The last time I spoke with my mum, I could tell by the tight tone in her voice that she was in a lot of pain. She would never tell me, so I relied on our neighbor, Louise, for updates. I send Louise a monthly stipend to keep an eye on Mum and Angelica and report back anything I need to know. Mum doesn't know about this arrangement, which I prefer. Louise lets me know when Angelica needs something or Mum's prescriptions are getting low or her electric bill too high. My mum fusses at me all the time for taking care of things, but I do it anyway. They're my family, and that says it all.

"Hello?"

My mum's voice greeted me as if she were down the block, not halfway around the world.

"Hi, Mum."

"Faith, my goodness. It's so good to hear from you. Shh, in a minute," she said to someone, most likely my sister.

"Faith, honey, how are you? Are you okay? Are you eating enough?"

I laughed. I could have scripted my mother's questions as if I'd said them myself. She asked the same questions every time I rang her. When we were together, she did the same, except for clucking her tongue and telling me I was too thin.

After reassuring her I was fit and full, we caught up for a few minutes as I walked down the corridor. I'd skip coffee any day for the chance to talk to my family.

"Faith, what's wrong?" my mum asked, catching me off guard.

"What?"

"Don't pretend you didn't hear me." I hadn't really, though my mind had drifted to Lowe.

"Nothing, Mum." I was never a good liar and certainly not to my mum. When I was younger I'd look above my head, fully expecting to see a flashing neon sign that said LIAR when I did.

"Do not lie to me, Faith Elisabeth Williams."

I knew I was in big trouble when my mum broke out my full name.

"Are you sick? Did you get fired?"

"No, Mum." I shook my head. Jeez. Why did she always jump to the worst conclusion?

"I just wanted to hear your voice." The instant after the words passed my lips, I knew that was the wrong thing to say.

"There is something wrong. Tell me."

I wondered if, when I had a child, I would have the same sixth sense as my mum has. Did that come with mum training, the same class that taught all mums to say no.

"It's nothing, Mum." My protest was weak.

"Do not tell me it's nothing. If it were, you'd not be ringing me."

"I met someone." I stopped, shocked at the words I'd just blurted out. I looked around to see if anyone had heard me. Anyone like Lowe.

"You don't sound happy about it."

I didn't reply. I didn't know what to say.

"What's her name?"

I looked around again for eavesdroppers. "Lowe Carter." A simple name, but there was nothing simple about her.

"You've never mentioned her before."

I could almost hear the wheels in my mum's head turning. "No, we, uh…met a couple of weeks ago." My mum didn't have to ask how someone I'd just met had become so important for me to utter those three words. How is it that "I met someone" said it all?

"Tell me about her," Mum asked, and for the next ten minutes I told her everything.

The way Lowe looked at me, the sound of her voice, the way she laughed, how her smile lit up my insides, how handsome she was in her tuxedo. My mum and I may be close, but I didn't share how her touch ignited me, my name whispered in the dark took my breath away. And I certainly didn't confess how she made me crazy with desire for her.

"She sounds like a wonderful person. So, what's the problem?"

"She's the daughter of a resident," I said quietly, even though no one was anywhere near me.

"I see." That was all my mum said. She knew the implications.

"Don't worry, Mum. It's just a thing."

"It doesn't sound like just a thing to me," she said, using my own words.

"It will be," I said, more to convince myself than my mum. "She leaves in a few days, and that will be that." More convincing.

"Faith, you need to—"

I didn't let my mum begin to tell me what I already knew. "I know, I know. Don't worry, Mum. It'll be all right. I'll be all right." I would be—eventually—maybe.

I spoke with Angelica, and after a few minutes, my mum came back on the line.

"I have to get to work, Mum." I hated lying to her, but I had to get off the phone before I started to cry at the unreasonableness of what I'd gotten myself into. I'd put myself here, and it was up to me to get myself out.

# Chapter Twenty-seven

*Day Nineteen*

After searching what felt like the entire ship yesterday, I found Faith sitting in a back booth of one of the restaurants. She had a pile of pristine white napkins in her lap and a tray of silverware on the table. My heart jumped with excitement, and my clit for the same reason.

Her back was to me, so I could watch her undetected for a few minutes. Her hair was up, exposing the back of her neck and that one little spot that, when I kissed it, made her moan with pleasure. The clip in her hair was the one I'd pulled out just before we fell into each other's arms.

She smoothed another napkin, and my mind flashed on her hands running up and down my legs, inching closer and closer to my center with each stroke. Her hands were strong, her fingers sure and confident.

My knees started to feel weak, and I needed to sit down. No one had ever affected me like Faith did. Sure, I'd thought about the women I'd slept with, but not nearly the constant, mind-consuming way I thought about Faith.

What was she doing? Who was she with? Was she thinking about me? Remembering, no, reliving our hours together? Was she planning how we could get together again? Without question, she'd enjoyed it. Dozens of orgasms don't lie.

I slowly approached, my rehearsed words on the tip of my tongue. When she turned around and our eyes met, I couldn't think or reason.

"Hi." God, what a stupid thing to say.

Faith looked over her shoulder before speaking. "Hello."

That was about all my brain could manage with Faith's dark, penetrating eyes on mine. I know what they looked like when she was happy, playful, bashful, and just before she came. I didn't know what they were expressing now.

"May I sit down?" I finally managed to say. I was uncharacteristically tongue-tied. Faith hesitated. "For just a minute," I added quickly.

"Certainly," she finally said, a little too stiffly.

I pulled out a chair adjacent to the table and sat down. "I've been looking for you."

"I've been busy."

"How are you?"

"Fine."

"Faith," I said.

"Lowe, you don't owe me anything. It was something we both wanted, and we had a good time. Nothing more, nothing less. I'm okay with it."

Well, I wasn't, so I pressed on. "That wasn't why I wanted to talk to you."

"It's not going to happen again," Faith said, quietly, looking over her shoulder. "It can't."

"Can't? What do you mean it can't?" I said a little too loudly. I quieted my voice when Faith looked like she was about to bolt. "Why can't we see each other again?" A nagging suspicion tickled the back of my neck. My stomach started churning. "You said you weren't involved with anyone."

"I'm not."

"Then what is it? You didn't seem to have a problem with it before." I didn't know whether to be hurt, angry, or disappointed.

"It's against the rules," she said simply.

"What rules?"

"Captain's rules."

"The captain said you can't have sex?"

"With residents."

"I'm not a resident."

"Or their guests."

What in the hell was going on here? When we'd been together, Faith couldn't keep her hands, and other equally skillful body parts, off me, and now, she was saying it's against the rules?

"Wait. Let me get this straight." I put my hands up, palms facing her. "The captain has a rule that members of the crew can't get involved with a resident or any of their guests?" When she nodded, I asked, "Why? We're all adults here." I was generally a rule follower, but this one was completely absurd.

"He said it causes trouble."

"And he doesn't want trouble on the ship," I interjected. "What happens if it happens?" My question sounded ridiculous, but Faith got the gist.

"We could be fired."

"Fired? As in fired? Can he do that? Is that even legal?"

"When we're in international waters he makes the rules. And it's ship policy"

"But we weren't in international waters," I reminded Faith. We had been very much on dry land.

"I know."

"Then what's the problem?"

"I don't want to have a vacation fling with you," Faith shot back, anger tinting her words.

"It sure didn't seem like that to me when you had your tongue down my throat and your fingers in—"

"Stop it." Faith's words were strong and harsh, her eyes blazing. "Don't you dare turn this into something it wasn't."

"I'm sorry," I said quickly, appropriately chastised. "I didn't mean it to come out that way. Our time together wasn't cheap or tawdry, and I, in no way, meant to imply it was." I sat back and ran my hand through my hair, trying to get ahold of my wayward emotions. "I just want to see you again." I sounded desperate and didn't care.

"It's not possible. Unlike the residents on this ship, I need this job. I can't risk—"

"What if we just saw each other when we're in port?" I was getting more and more desperate as the minutes ticked by. Faith frowned, apparently confused. I saw my opening and jumped in. "If the rule is no shipboard romances, then there should be nothing wrong with a land-based one." It sounded pretty good to me.

"I don't think that's exactly what he meant," Faith said.

"What if we—"

Faith's eyes blazed again. "I am not going to ask the captain, who just happens to be about four levels of management above me, if it would be okay if I have sex with the daughter of the owners of 1504, but only when we're on land. Did I get that right?"

It did sound a little silly when she said it, and I told her so.

"Silly? You think it would be silly? Try ridiculous, ludicrous, bizarre, and absolutely absurd."

"But, if we—"

"There is no 'but,' Lowe. Don't you get it? Just because your parents are on this ship does not mean you get whatever you want."

"My parents have nothing to do with this," I fired back, angry that they had been brought into the conversation.

"Don't they?" Faith asked in disbelief. "They own one of the best apartments on the ship, and with that comes certain expected perks, but I'm not one of them."

"Yes, you've told me that several times. Actually, I think you said you weren't an amenity."

"Nor will I be their daughter's plaything just because you're bored."

That statement threw me and felt like a slap in the face. I was so stunned I wasn't able to say anything as Faith stood and walked away.

# CHAPTER TWENTY-EIGHT

*Day 22*
*At sea*
*Sydney to Fiji*

More than a little exhausted, I stumbled up the stairs. It was after eight our second day at sea after departing Sydney Harbor. I was scheduled for the sun deck, and it would be good for me to get some fresh air and sun.

I was straightening the freshly laundered towels on the shelf when a wave of awareness came over me and a shiver ran down my spine. My hands started to tremble, and my heart pounded. Only one person had ever caused a reaction like this, but she wasn't supposed to be standing behind me in the middle of the Tasman Sea.

"Hello, Faith."

The sound of her saying my name made my knees weak. It took me back to the dozens of other times she'd whispered it or called it out in a moment of passion.

"What are you doing here?" I was afraid to turn around. It was four days after I left her on the deck, and I'd finally gotten myself together, so I didn't have to struggle to breathe.

"Looking for you."

"I thought you left."

"Apparently not."

"Why not?" I asked but was scared to death to learn the reason.

"Not that I'm complaining about the view, but are you going to look at me?"

I spun around, realizing she was probably staring at my butt. She'd told me over and over how she thought it was perfect.

My pulse jumped. Lowe was the best-looking thing I'd seen since walking away from her the day before we docked in Sydney. The day she was supposed to fly to the other side of the world, go on with her life, and release me from her spell.

She was more striking and overwhelmingly captivating than I remembered. The pull between us was powerful, and I had to use all my willpower not be swept into it. Lowe's eyes were piercing, and I was sure she could see right through me.

"I don't like unfinished business."

My heart leapt again. We were unfinished business?

"Why are you hiding from me?"

"I didn't know you'd stayed aboard." That was true, but it sounded like a weak excuse.

"I looked for you everywhere."

She'd looked for me? "It's a big ship."

Lowe raised her eyebrows like she'd caught me in a fib. "Why are you here?" I asked.

Please, please, please say it's because you can't live without me, I thought. That you can't stop thinking about me. That you dream about a life with me raising kids in a big house with a couple of dogs. That you can't breathe without me in your life. That the sun shines brighter, the air is cleaner, and the world is a better place with me beside you.

"Why did you walk away?"

I glanced around the pool, looking for an escape. I wanted to run, sprint from my chaotic emotions.

"I had to get to work."

"That's not what I'm talking about, and you know it." Her words were strong. I wondered if that was her boss voice.

"You were leaving. We had a good time, and it was over. You were going home in two days. What was the point?"

*Please don't say what I desperately want you to. I don't have the strength to step away again.*

"So that's it then?"

"What else is there?" *Other than the fact that Raul thinks I'm in love with you. He tried to convince me of it last night.*

*"You're in love with her," Raul said after I spilled my guts to him. We were in my room, a half-eaten, his half, pizza between us. My appetite had disappeared around the time I took my clothes off in front of Lowe and now, three days later, had still not returned. I'd managed to avoid her the two days we were at sea returning to Sydney. We'd docked earlier this morning, and if I could just stay out of sight until we departed this evening, I wouldn't have to risk running into her again.*

*"I am not in love with her," I replied adamantly. I couldn't be. We'd spent, what, a few weeks together? We barely knew each other.*

*"Don't lie to yourself, Faith."*

*"I'm not." God, I sounded pathetic. "I admit I fell for her, but it was purely physical. I did not fall in love with her." Absolutely no way. Maybe if I said it a hundred times more, I'd begin to believe it.*

*"What would be the point?" I asked, unable to stop myself. Raul just sat patiently listening to me. "She left to go home, and we're headed to Fiji, for crying out loud. She won't be back for another year."*

*"Love doesn't always follow the rules," Raul said patiently.*

*"Stop saying that," I barked. I cringed at his hurt expression.*

*"Okay, okay, whatever you say."*

*He finally stopped talking nonsense and changed the subject. At least I think he did, for my thoughts and attention had drifted back to Lowe.*

Lowe looked intense. I could see her thoughts churning in her head. It felt like forever before the expression on her face hardened.

"Maybe I wanted to spend more time with you?"

"Again, what was the point? It's not like we're building a relationship and are going to date or spend the rest of our lives together."

Lowe's eyes flared, and I tried to laugh off the idea, but it sounded more like I was choking.

I was trying to be loose and easy about our time together. Isn't that what a rich, successful woman like Lowe wanted? She wasn't looking for happily ever after. It was obvious what her parents thought of me. Even though Lowe was her own woman, could she go against them on something so important? My family meant the world to me, and I refused to put her in that position.

"Excuse me, Ms. Carter."

Rob, one of the deck hands, interrupted us. I wasn't sure if I was grateful or wanted to push him overboard.

"Ms. Carter," he asked again since Lowe hadn't acknowledged him.

"Yes?" She was still looking at me.

"I have a note from your parents." He handed Lowe a folded sheet of white paper. I caught a glimpse of the *Escape* logo on the top.

"Thank you," she replied, not taking her eyes off me.

Rob hesitated, obviously not sure what he was supposed to do. He glanced from Lowe to me.

"Thanks, Rob," I said, giving him an approving nod. He scampered away, but not before looking between Lowe and me again. I was sure we'd be the talk of the crew by dinner.

"It seems as though you've already made up your mind about us," Lowe said after he was out of earshot.

"I think it's pretty obvious we have no future," I somehow managed to say.

Lowe's eyes were hard and probing, and I felt pinned to the deck. *Don't look away, and for God's sake, don't let her see how devastated you are.* I told myself this several times before Lowe finally stood. She didn't say anything as she walked away.

My heart crashed, and I wanted to curl up into a ball until the stabbing pain subsided. I would always ache, but I could live with that. I'd have to.

## Chapter Twenty-nine

My resolve hardened. Faith was lying. I could see it written all over her face. She wore her emotions like an outer skin. What we had shared these past few weeks meant something to her, regardless of her words to the contrary. I'd extended my departure and had a week to make her realize it, yet I had no idea how. But then what? We'd sail off into the sunset? Pretty corny considering we were on a ship. It wasn't very feasible either. What would I do? Sell my business and move in with my parents to be with Faith? I certainly couldn't afford to buy a place on the *Escape*. Would Faith quit her job and come home to Phoenix with me? She'd be crazy to do that. She didn't know me any more than I knew her. Making a commitment like that didn't make sense. Besides, was I ready for that?

My head was pounding when I met my parents for dinner later that evening. They'd insisted, even though I knew we had nothing more to talk about. We'd both made our respective points clear the day before we docked in Sydney.

*"I've decided to stay on until Hawaii, if that's all right with you."*

*Both my parents and my sister stopped eating, their forks halfway to their mouths. They looked comical. Three sets of eyes turned my way. That rarely happened.*

*"I don't think that's a good idea," my mother said, setting her fork on the table next to her plate and delicately wiping the corners of her lipsticked mouth with her linen napkin.*

*At that moment, I was certain she knew about Faith. "Why do you say that?" I knew what her answer would be, but for some masochistic reason I needed to hear it.*

*"I don't think I need to explain."*

*"Yes, Mother, you do. I'd like to know why you disapprove of your daughter's happiness so much." Not that it mattered. It hadn't for a very long time.*

*"Lowe," Victoria said, but I cut her off before she had a chance to say any more.*

*"I'm not talking to you, Victoria."*

*The room was quiet as I waited for my mother to answer my question. My father hadn't said anything, not that I expected him to. Amazingly, Victoria kept her mouth shut.*

*"All right, Lowe," Mother said. "That girl is not our kind. She is not up to the level with which we choose to associate. For God's sake, she works for us," she said with emphasis. "If you want to have a casual affair, then please keep it to yourself. We do not parade around with the help, and we certainly don't marry them." The tone of her voice was as distasteful as the words she'd spoken. Victoria nodded in smug agreement.*

*"We forbid it," she added, as if her words were the eleventh commandment.*

*"You...you forbid it?" I asked, shocked at the snobbery and audacity of her words.*

*"Yes. We will not have you—"*

*I calmly folded my napkin and laid it on the table beside my crystal water glass. "I'm a grown woman, and I've been making my own decisions for many years. You have not dictated anything about my life since I was eighteen years old, and I will not allow you to start now." I stood and pushed my chair in. "I'll have the purser collect my things within the hour." I walked out of my parents' apartment knowing I'd never step foot inside it again.*

The hostess showed me to their table, and I sat down. My greeting was polite, yet cold.

My father's cocktail glass was almost empty, and my mother's expression was pinched. Somehow, I'd escaped the ordeal of Victoria in attendance as well.

Our waitress, who, thank God wasn't Faith, appeared almost immediately, and I ordered a double Crown and Coke. I might not be at the table long, and I'd definitely need it.

My parents perused their menu like this was a normal, everyday family dinner. I had no appetite but needed something to occupy my hands and attention. I couldn't make out the items in small print and realized my hands were shaking. I laid my menu on the table and folded my hands over it.

My drink arrived, and our server probably could sense the tension between us and left us alone. I waited for either the inquisition or the lecture to begin. It wouldn't be long.

"Have you given any thought to our recent conversation?" my mother asked. Her tone was so matter-of-fact, she could have been asking if I'd decided where we should have lunch tomorrow.

"I think moving to one of the guest suites signaled my intentions," I replied, sipping my cocktail. Captain Waverly hadn't asked when he gave me the card key to apartment 805. My mother's face didn't move, but I saw a slight tic in the corner of her right eye. She was pissed. I'd never gone against her wishes since I'd never had a strong-enough reason to. Until now. Faith was walking into the restaurant on the arm of Theodore Blackwell.

Faith looked amazing. She was wearing the same black dress she'd worn to the Cobalt party, but she had accessorized it with a brightly colored scarf around her neck, a wide gold belt, and a pair of casual sandals. Her hair was down, a bangle of bracelets on her left wrist.

She had yet to see me, and I watched the hostess lead them to their table on the other side of the room. Mr. Blackwell held her chair, and after she settled in and looked up, our eyes met.

The air between us sizzled like an energized electrical line. My breathing turned shallow and my insides into mush. She was beautiful, and I wished I was the one sitting across from her.

"Are you even listening to me, Lowe?"

Hearing my name drew my attention away from Faith. "Obviously not, Mother. What did you say?" I really didn't care. It would be more of the same, and I wasn't interested and didn't even want to waste my time listening to her.

"I said we think you're making a big mistake. Your father and I have taught you the difference between right and wrong and the importance of character in our family. We expected more from you." The past tense signaled their profound disappointment.

I looked between her and my father, a sudden sadness filling my bones. I hadn't lived up to their standards. A mirror sense of their failure as my parents, whose only concern should be the happiness of their child, flooded me. Why did it matter who I loved as long I was loved in return? What was so important that overrode my euphoria at finding the woman I wanted to spend the rest of my life with? Who was to say Faith couldn't be a part of this family, my family? Where was it written that my parents should determine my future?

Nothing, no one, and nowhere, which is exactly where we were right now. We weren't at an impasse. I'd made my decision and was moving on, either with or without them in my life. I folded my napkin neatly and placed it on my menu.

"I'm sorry you're disappointed in me," I said, careful not to use the phrase "I'm sorry I disappointed you." It was a subtle, yet distinct difference. "But I'm going to live my life the way I see fit and have people in it who love and support me. If that's not you, then I truly am sorry." I rose from the table, walked away, and didn't look back.

❖

My dinner with Mr. B was a bust. I'd been looking forward to it all afternoon, but the minute I saw Lowe across the dining room, my heart lurched, and I just wanted to crawl under the table and not come out until the pain disappeared. We were arriving in Fiji the day after tomorrow, then five days to Hawaii after that. I had no idea how long she would be on board, and if I kept reacting like this, I'd be a complete mess by the time she did leave.

I tried to pay attention to Mr. B. He was a sweet guy and always had a lot of interesting things to say, but I couldn't focus. I could see Lowe directly over his left shoulder, and my eyes kept drifting to her. She didn't look happy, and I wondered what she and her parents were talking about. They should be thrilled that she'd stayed on, but it certainly didn't look like it.

Suddenly, Lowe rose from the table, pushed her chair in, and walked away. She looked shaken, and instead of heading directly for the exit, she detoured our way. The closer she got to our table, the more relaxed she appeared.

"Good evening, Mr. Blackwell, Faith," she said, greeting us both. "I don't mean to intrude, but I just wanted to stop by and say hello and invite you to a poker game tomorrow on deck twelve," Lowe said, directing her invitation to Mr. B.

"Poker? I love poker," Mr. B. said excitedly. "Absolutely. What time?"

"One thirty. No money. Just bragging rights."

Lowe smiled at him and laid her hand casually on his shoulder. She was completely focused on Mr. B., and he came alive under the attention. She turned to me. "You're welcome too, Faith."

The pull of her gaze was powerful, and it almost sucked me in. She was looking at me intently, and I needed to remember our situation. "Thanks, but I've got plans." I did have plans. Tomorrow was my day off, and I'd decided to stay in my room and wallow in self-pity.

"Well, if you change your mind, you know where we'll be. You two have a nice dinner."

Lowe looked at me again for a long moment, then walked away.

"She's so friendly," Mr. B. said, smiling.

"Yes, she is," I replied.

"She's so unlike her sister and her parents." He looked around like a spy passing on secret information. "I don't mean to talk ill of people, but her sister is a snob. Takes after her mother. They're awful. Just because I don't own an apartment on their floor, I'm not worth their time." He tsked. "People like that should be brought down a peg or two."

It was easier to pay attention with Lowe out of the room, and I did my best to be an enjoyable, engaged dinner companion. I don't know what we talked about, but it was nothing heavy. Finally, he called it a night, and I was able to leave.

I was too keyed up to sleep, so I strolled around the deck. As I approached the pool I saw a figure lying in one of the lounge chairs. As I got closer, I recognized it was Lowe. She hadn't seen me yet, so I had the opportunity to turn around before she did. I kept moving forward.

"How was your dinner?" Lowe asked as I approached.

"It was good, and the company enjoyable. Mr. B. is a sweet man."

"I heard he lost his wife not too long ago."

"It's been almost a year," I replied.

"It was nice of you to have dinner with him."

"Nice has nothing to do with it. I enjoy his company."

The air between us was still. My heart, on the other hand, was pounding.

"Would you like to sit?" Lowe motioned to the chair to her left.

I knew I shouldn't, but I pulled it over and sat down.

## CHAPTER THIRTY

I was more than a little surprised when Faith agreed to join me. I thought for sure she'd make some excuse, and when she pulled the chair close, a star twinkled above me. We sat silently for some time, a meteor shower blanketing the sky overhead. I was calm, a complete shift of my emotions after the few minutes with my parents. I was still hurt and angry, but those feelings were much less prominent with Faith beside me. A vague recollection of our first day together when I'd joked with Faith about how I needed her beside me, especially when I visited my parents, had come true.

"How are your parents?"

"Disappointed."

"In what?"

"Me." Faith turned and looked at me.

"You? What did you do?"

"Didn't get off the ship in Sydney."

"Excuse me?" Faith said, clearly confused.

"They're upset that I stayed on board."

"Why?"

"Because I fell for a beautiful, charming, smart, sexy, exciting, desirable woman who happens to work here. She's a bit younger than I am, and that, in and of itself, could be scandalous in my parents' circle. She's delightful, funny, thoughtful, and takes care of her family. Her eyes are the color of ebony when she's mad and burning embers when she's aroused. She's considerate, attentive, passionate, silly, and the best damn kisser I've ever known. She's captivating, mesmerizing, and has fascinated me from the moment we met."

Faith didn't move. I don't think she even breathed. I hadn't meant to spring it on her like that, but it just came out. I couldn't stop. I didn't want to.

I swung my legs over the side of the chair and faced her. I tried to chuckle. "My BFF Charlotte always says go big or go home."

Finally, Faith spoke, her voice barely a whisper, "Well, you certainly accomplished one of them."

I took several deep breaths, preparing to jump into a place I've never been, where joy and happiness overflowed and beauty and ecstasy stretched as far as I can see. It was a place where time stood still and the future rushed forward at the same time, a situation where I had no idea what to do or how to do it, but I did know I couldn't possibly back out now. I leapt. "I've fallen for you, Faith."

Faith wouldn't look at me, but I could see the muscles in her jaw working.

"That's two go-bigs," she said hesitantly.

"Yeah, well…I, uh…didn't mean to drop it in your lap like this, but—"

"When did you intend to?"

I detected a hint of anger in her voice. "I hadn't actually gotten that far. It probably would have been over a nice dinner or a glass of wine on the deck. Something a little more romantic or private."

"And what am I supposed to do with this information?"

I wasn't expecting this reaction, regardless of the setting. I'd thought she'd at least say she felt something for me. At least I'd hoped she would.

The longer we sat there, the more I began to realize I might be wrong, very wrong. Faith looked everywhere but at me.

"I don't know, Faith. I guess I was hoping you kind of liked me back," I finally said. I winced at the childishness of my words. I was trying to ease some of the tension between us with humor, but it appeared I had failed.

She turned to me, her facial expression not what I expected. I saw anguish in her eyes, and fear. My heart suddenly ached for putting it there.

"And we'd do what? Row into the sunset and live happily ever after?" She fisted her hands, squinted her eyes shut, and frowned like she had a bad headache. Her eyes opened, and she whipped her head around to face me again. "You don't even know me. It's not going to happen."

I barely had a chance to get my legs out of the way as she stood and then hurried across the deck and through a pair of green doors.

# CHAPTER THIRTY-ONE

*Day 26*
*Malolo, Fiji*

Sand tickled the bottom of my bare feet as I crossed a gently curved wooden bridge spanning crystal-clear water to reach my cabana. I'd gotten the place after another guest at the Likuliki Lagoon Resort had canceled at the last minute. A tender had taken me to Malolo Island earlier this afternoon, leaving behind my parents and Faith. If only my tangled emotions were as easy. As I approached the grass-thatched building, I found it ironic that the seclusion I needed to clear my head was that which was highly sought after by lovers.

Green grass covered most of the man-made petite island, trees and native plants creating plenty of shade. Four steps led to a patio with a fabulous view of the bay. I stepped inside. The floor was polished to a sheen that reflected the mid-afternoon sun. Four-inch wooden shutters covered every window, most of which were open, allowing the breeze to float through the long, narrow room. It reminded me of those advertisements on Facebook about the perfect private vacation spot. I dropped my bag at the foot of the bed and, after dropping my shoes onto the floor and grabbing a bottle of water from the stocked refrigerator, headed to the front patio.

Several hours later I had yet to figure out what I was going to do. I was still reeling from my conversation with my father this morning.

*"Sleep well?"*

*My father sat down beside me, his long, tanned legs filling the length of the chaise by the pool. His deck shoes looked brand-new.*

*"For the most part, yes," I said honestly. I'd tossed and turned and fretted about my feelings for Faith and my family's very vocal disapproval.*

*The silence between us was uncomfortable. I sensed that my father had something more to say, and I wasn't sure I wanted to hear it. Everyone had made their view as clear as the water in the pool. I'd seen a very different side of them this trip, and quite frankly, I didn't like it, or them. I'd never be friends with my sister, and my mother, well, she was at an entirely different level of disapproval.*

*The realization that this would be my last trip filled me more with relief than sadness. I'd obviously keep in touch, but my visits going forward would be brief and in a location where they were in port. I'd fly there, visit for a few days, then take my own vacation. I felt as if a suffocating blanket had been lifted off my shoulders. The air was cleaner, the sun brighter.*

*"I want you to be happy, Lowe, and if Faith is the woman who makes you feel that way, then I'm happy for you."*

*His words stunned me. My father had never talked to me about my love for women. It was just something we never spoke about. He'd barely acknowledged it when I told them on Christmas break my senior year in college and dropped the bombshell that had changed our lives. My mother had been livid, Victoria more worried that her friends would think she was queer, and my father still hadn't recovered from my announcement earlier in the day that I was not going on to law school.*

*Now he was what? Giving me his blessing? He had never, ever, ever gone against anything my mother said. Holy shit.*

*"I beg your pardon?" That was all I could say. I needed a minute to process.*

*"You heard me," he said, his gaze never leaving the water. "Life is too short to live it unhappy. If you've learned nothing from me, please learn this."*

*He left me alone on the deck, but not before laying his hand gently on my shoulder for several seconds.*

*I had no idea how long I sat there in complete disbelief.*

I cared about Faith, deeply. No, that was bullshit. I was in love with her, and I had to have her in my life. She made me laugh, think, and live. I'd only thought I was happy. With Faith I was alive. She made me soar with happiness. Whoever said that giving is better than getting must have been talking about making love with the woman you love. With her by my side I could accomplish anything, but if for some reason I couldn't, I wanted her beside me to pick up the pieces and help me move on.

But she didn't want me. I had thick skin, but this realization almost knocked me to my knees. Nausea threatened to send me to the bushes, but I tapped it down from sheer will. I had to go on. I had a thriving business I loved, good friends, and a full life.

At least I'd thought I had a full life until I met Faith. Now I just felt empty, like the hollow pit in my stomach. I'd go home and pick up where I'd left off, but it wouldn't be the same. The famous line of poetry from Alfred Lord Tennyson about it being better to love and lose than never try it barged into my head. What complete and total bullshit.

❖

"Earth to Faith."

Raul's voice penetrated the fog that had been my constant companion ever since I'd left Lowe on the deck what felt like just yesterday.

I'd run from Lowe both literally and figuratively. Her declaration had come out of nowhere, and I wasn't prepared. I didn't know what to do. No one had ever reached into my soul the way Lowe had, and I was scared. Plain and simple, I was scared to death.

Raul and I were eating breakfast at one of the small coffee shops on deck nine. We'd docked in Malolo during the night. My tired, bloodshot eyes were in constant motion for any sign of Lowe. She was the last thing I needed this morning.

"Tell me, chica," Raul said, his voice gentle and encouraging. I told Raul the entire story.

"You had to have known something was up," he said like I was an idiot. "Why else would she have stayed?"

"I don't know. Maybe because her family is here?" I barked, not sparing the sarcasm. "Jeez, I'm sorry, Raul." I laid my hand on top of his. "I'm just so messed up. I don't know what to do."

I'd bounced back and forth, trying to get my head around my feelings for Lowe. Her revelation certainly didn't help. We were in a no-win situation.

"It's not like we live on different sides of the country," I explained needlessly. "Or even different countries, for that matter. That wouldn't be ideal but still doable."

"Planes fly all over the world, Faith."

"I know, but this is different," I said, but a nagging ping began in the back of my brain. "Don't ask me to explain it. It just is." I'd lost my patience and my equilibrium just thinking about it.

"Have you talked to her?"

"About what?" I asked, exasperated at Raul and his constant questions I didn't have the answers to.

"About how you two can make it work."

"Who says I want to make it work?"

Raul raised his eyebrows and stared at me like I'd lost my mind along with my heart.

"Don't look at me like that."

He didn't change his expression or the tilt of his head. Does everybody hate their BFF when they're right?

Thirty minutes later, I steeled myself, lifted my head, squared my shoulders, and knocked on the door. My heart was racing, and my fight-or-flight response was in full debate. I had raised my hand to knock again when the door swung open.

"Good afternoon, Mr. Carter. Is Lowe in?"

I wish I could read minds as Lowe's father studied me. What did he see? A worker on his ship? Someone of a lower class than he? A gold digger? An opportunist? A woman not too proud to go after what she wanted? The woman who loved his daughter?

"No, I'm afraid she's not," he said finally.

"Landon, who is it?" I heard Mrs. Carter ask over his shoulder.

"No one, Francis," he replied.

My heart sank, and my stomach plummeted. Nausea gripped my gut, and I was afraid I might be sick. That would be perfect. I turned to leave, proverbial tail tucked between my legs.

"Faith, wait." He stepped into the hall, closing the door slightly.

As much as I wanted to take my humiliation and run away, I didn't.

"Lowe moved out. She's in room 805." He paused. "I'm sure she'd want to see you."

What was he saying? Why was he telling me where she was? Didn't Lowe's family think I wasn't good enough for their daughter? They'd made it pretty clear to me. My stomach started to drift back to its original position, and my heart started beating again.

"Thank you," I said, my voice firm.

"Don't make me sorry I told you."

"No sir. I won't."

## CHAPTER THIRTY-TWO

W hat do you mean she's not here?" I'd looked everywhere on the ship for Lowe after she didn't answer her door. I'd run into Caroline, one of the pursers.

"Just what I said. She went to shore on one of the tenders this afternoon."

"Do you know where she went?"

Carolyn looked at me, then asked, "I thought you were finished with your personal tour-guide assignment." Her insinuation was clear.

"That's not what this is about. Do you know where she went?" I asked again.

"What is it about?" she asked, frowning. She obviously knew and did not approve. What was it with people? Doesn't everyone deserve to be happy? I needed to find another way to get the information I desperately needed. I toned my eagerness down a few notches.

"Nothing. It can wait until she gets back. Thank you." I hurried off in search of the one individual who just might know. I'd made many friends on the *Escape*, some of whom owed me a favor or three, and I called in my markers.

The tender left me in front of a weathered bridge that led to my future. I had nothing in my hands as I walked across the hard deck. Once I found out where Lowe was staying, I hadn't stopped to grab anything other than my shoulder bag.

I barely noticed the clear water under my feet or the birds in the trees as I approached the bungalow. I was looking for Lowe.

She was sitting in a chair on the patio and was the most beautiful thing I'd ever seen. My heart raced even faster, pounding against my chest, and the butterflies in my stomach did somersaults. I had never been so scared. I had absolutely no idea what I was going to say. I had no plans other than to follow her lead wherever it took us. I wanted us to be a cliché, where she swept me off my feet and carried me to the bed. I wanted to touch her, hold her, hear her heart beat in time with mine. I needed to have her arms around me, feel her body pressed against mine, her hands and mouth on me again, breathe her air.

Each step brought me closer to Lowe, and when our eyes met, the world started turning again. A knot formed in my throat, and I couldn't speak.

Seconds passed in what felt like hours as neither of us spoke. Wasn't my showing up here explanation enough? Didn't the fact that I was risking everything provide enough words of commitment? I suddenly realized she was waiting for me to verbalize what I wanted. She'd already confessed her feelings. It was now my turn.

"I don't know what I'm doing here other than I can't stop thinking about you. I can't stop thinking about how you make me feel and how I feel when I'm not with you. I don't know how I'd live without you, and I don't want to try. I realize your family doesn't approve of me, and I'd never stand between you and your parents. Family means everything, and I'd never take that away from you. I said you didn't know anything about me," I said before my nerves fizzled. "I don't know everything about you either." I took the biggest breath of my life. "But I want to spend a lifetime learning."

"Faith."

"I know I've been hot and cold and probably driving you crazy. I don't know anything about your business or Arizona but—"

"Faith," Lowe repeated, louder when I didn't stop talking.

"What?" I had at least thirty more reasons I was ready to convey to convince Lowe just how much I loved her and wanted to make a life with her.

Lowe stood and calmly walked over and stopped, inches from me. She broke into a grin, her eyes sparkling, then flaming with desire.

"Shut up and kiss me."

THE END

# About the Author

Julie Cannon divides her time by being a corporate suit, a wife, mom, sister, friend, and writer. Julie and her wife have lived in at least a half a dozen states, traveled around the world, and have an unending supply of dedicated friends. And of course, the most important people in their lives are their three kids, #1, Dude and the Devine Miss Em.

With the release of *Shut Up and Kiss Me*, Julie will have eighteen books published by Bold Strokes Books. Her first novel, *Come and Get Me*, was a finalist for the Golden Crown Literary Society's Best Lesbian Romance and Debut Author Awards and *I Remember* won the GCLS Best Lesbian Romance in 2014. *Rescue Me* and *Wishing on a Dream* were finalists for Best Lesbian Romance from the prestigious Lambda Literary Society.

www.JulieCannon.com

# Books Available from Bold Strokes Books

**A Chapter on Love** by Laney Webber. When Jannika and Lee reunite, their instant connection feels like a gift, but neither is ready for a second chance at love. Will they finally get on the same page when it comes to love? (978-1-63555-366-6)

**Drawing Down the Mist** by Sheri Lewis Wohl. Everyone thinks Grand Duchess Maria Romanova died in 1918. They were almost right. (978-1-63555-341-3)

**Listen** by Kris Bryant. Lily Croft is inexplicably drawn to Hope D'Marco but will she have the courage to confront the consequences of her past and present colliding? (978-1-63555-318-5)

**Perfect Partners** by Maggie Cummings. Elite police dog trainer Sara Wright has no intention of falling in love with a coworker, until Isabel Marquez arrives at Homeland Security's Northeast Regional Training facility and Sara's good intentions start to falter. (978-1-63555-363-5)

**Shut Up and Kiss Me** by Julie Cannon. What better way to spend two weeks of hell in paradise than in the company of a hot, sexy woman? (978-1-63555-343-7)

**Spencer's Cove** by Missouri Vaun. When Foster Owen and Abigail Spencer meet they uncover a story of lives adrift, loves lost, and true love found. (978-1-63555-171-6)

**Without Pretense** by TJ Thomas. After living for decades hiding from the truth, can Ava learn to trust Bianca with her secrets and her heart? (978-1-63555-173-0)

**Unexpected Lightning** by Cass Sellars. Lightning strikes once more when Sydney and Parker fight a dangerous stranger who threatens the peace they both desperately want. (978-1-163555-276-8)

**Emily's Art and Soul** by Joy Argento. When Emily meets Andi Marino she thinks she's found a new best friend but Emily doesn't know that Andi is fast falling in love with her. Caught up in exploring her sexuality, will Emily see the only woman she needs is right in front of her? (978-1-63555-355-0)

**Escape to Pleasure: Lesbian Travel Erotica** edited by Sandy Lowe and Victoria Villasenor. Join these award-winning authors as they explore the sensual side of erotic lesbian travel. (978-1-63555-339-0)

**Music City Dreamers** by Robyn Nyx. Music can bring lovers together. In Music City, it can tear them apart. (978-1-63555-207-2)

**Ordinary is Perfect** by D. Jackson Leigh. Atlanta marketing superstar Autumn Swan's life derails when she inherits a country home, a child, and a very interesting neighbor. (978-1-63555-280-5)

**Royal Court** by Jenny Frame. When royal dresser Holly Weaver's passionate personality begins to melt Royal Marine Captain Quincy's icy heart, will Holly be ready for what she exposes beneath? (978-1-63555-290-4)

**Strings Attached** by Holly Stratimore. Success. Riches. Music. Passion. It's a life most can only dream of, but stardom comes at a cost. (978-1-63555-347-5)

**The Ashford Place** by Jean Copeland. When Isabelle Ashford inherits an old house in small-town Connecticut, family secrets, a shocking discovery, and an unexpected romance complicate her plan for a fast profit and a temporary stay. (978-1-63555-316-1)

**Treason** by Gun Brooke. Zoem Malderyn's existence is a deadly threat to everyone on Gemocon and Commander Neenja KahSandra must find a way to save the woman she loves from having to commit the ultimate sacrifice. (978-1-63555-244-7)

**A Wish Upon a Star** by Jeannie Levig. Erica Cooper has learned to depend on only herself, but when her new neighbor, Leslie Raymond, befriends Erica's special needs daughter, the walls protecting her heart threaten to crumble. (978-1-63555-274-4)

**Answering the Call** by Ali Vali. Detective Sept Savoie returns to the streets of New Orleans, as do the dead bodies from ritualistic killings, and she does everything in her power to bring them to justice while trying to keep her partner, Keegan Blanchard, safe. (978-1-63555-050-4)

**Breaking Down Her Walls** by Erin Zak. Could a love worth staying for be the key to breaking down Julia Finch's walls? (978-1-63555-369-7)

**Exit Plans for Teenage Freaks** by 'Nathan Burgoine. Cole always has a plan—especially for escaping his small-town reputation as "that kid who was kidnapped when he was four"—but when he teleports to a museum, it's time to face facts: it's possible he's a total freak after all. (978-1-63555-098-6)

**Friends Without Benefits** by Dena Blake. When Dex Putman gets the woman she thought she always wanted, she soon wonders if it's really love after all. (978-1-63555-349-9)

**Invalid Evidence** by Stevie Mikayne. Private Investigator Jil Kidd is called away to investigate a possible killer whale, just when her partner Jess needs her most. (978-1-63555-307-9)

**Pursuit of Happiness** by Carsen Taite. When attorney Stevie Palmer's client reveals a scandal that could derail Senator Meredith Mitchell's presidential bid, their chance at love may be collateral damage. (978-1-63555-044-3)

**Seascape** by Karis Walsh. Marine biologist Tess Hansen returns to Washington's isolated northern coast where she struggles to adjust to small-town living while courting an endowment for her orca research center from Brittany James. (978-1-63555-079-5)

**Second in Command** by VK Powell. Jazz Perry's life is disrupted and her career jeopardized when she becomes personally involved with the case of an abandoned child and the child's competent but strict social worker, Emory Blake. (978-1-63555-185-3)

**Taking Chances** by Erin McKenzie. When Valerie Cruz and Paige Wellington clash over what's in the best interest of the children in Valerie's care, the children may be the ones who teach them it's worth taking chances for love. (978-1-63555-209-6)

**All of Me** by Emily Smith. When chief surgical resident Galen Burgess meets her new intern, Rowan Duncan, she may finally discover that doing what you've always done will only give you what you've always had. (978-1-63555-321-5)

**As the Crow Flies** by Karen F. Williams. Romance seems to be blooming all around, but problems arise when a restless ghost emerges from the ether to roam the dark corners of this haunting tale. (978-1-63555-285-0)

**Both Ways** by Ileandra Young. SPEAR agent Danika Karson races to protect the city from a supernatural threat and must rely on the woman she's trained to despise: Rayne, an achingly beautiful vampire. (978-1-63555-298-0)

**Calendar Girl** by Georgia Beers. Forced to work together, Addison Fairchild and Kate Cooper discover that opposites really do attract. (978-1-63555-333-8)

**Lovebirds** by Lisa Moreau. Two women from different worlds collide in a small California mountain town, each with a mission that doesn't include falling in love. (978-1-63555-213-3)

**Media Darling** by Fiona Riley. Can Hollywood bad girl Emerson and reluctant celebrity gossip reporter Hayley work together to make each other's dreams come true? Or will Emerson's secrets ruin not one career, but two? (978-1-63555-278-2)

**Stroke of Fate** by Renee Roman. Can Sean Moore live up to her reputation and save Jade Rivers from the stalker determined to end Jade's career and, ultimately, her life? (978-1-63555-62-4)

**The Rise of the Resistance** by Jackie D. The soul of America has been lost for almost a century. A few people may be the difference between a phoenix rising to save the masses or permanent destruction. (978-1-63555-259-1)

**The Sex Therapist Next Door** by Meghan O'Brien. At the intersection of sex and intimacy, anything is possible. Even love. (978-1-63555-296-6)

**Unforgettable** by Elle Spencer. When one night changes a lifetime... Two romance novellas from best-selling author Elle Spencer. (978-1-63555-429-8)

**Against All Odds** by Kris Bryant, Maggie Cummings, M. Ullrich. Peyton and Tory escaped death once, but will they survive when Bradley's determined to make his kill rate one hundred percent? (978-1-63555-193-8)

**Autumn's Light** by Aurora Rey. Casual hookups aren't supposed to include romantic dinners and meeting the family. Can Mat Pero see beyond the heartbreak that led her to keep her worlds so separate, and will Graham Connor be waiting if she does? (978-1-63555-272-0)

**Breaking the Rules** by Larkin Rose. When Virginia and Carmen are thrown together by an embarrassing mistake they find out their stubborn determination isn't so heroic after all. (978-1-63555-261-4)

**Broad Awakening** by Mickey Brent. In the sequel to *Underwater Vibes*, Hélène and Sylvie find ruts in their road to eternal bliss. (978-1-63555-270-6)

**Broken Vows** by MJ Williamz. Sister Mary Margaret must reconcile her divided heart or risk losing a love that just might be heaven sent. (978-1-63555-022-1)

**Flesh and Gold** by Ann Aptaker. Havana, 1952, where art thief and smuggler Cantor Gold dodges gangland bullets and mobsters' schemes while she searches Havana's steamy Red Light district for her kidnapped love. (978-1-63555-153-2)

**Isle of Broken Years** by Jane Fletcher. Spanish noblewoman Catalina de Valasco is in peril, even before the pirates holding her for ransom sail into seas destined to become known as the Bermuda Triangle. (978-1-63555-175-4)

**Love Like This** by Melissa Brayden. Hadley Cooper and Spencer Adair set out to take the fashion world by storm. If only they knew their hearts were about to be taken. (978-1-63555-018-4)

**Secrets On the Clock** by Nicole Disney. Jenna and Danielle love their jobs helping endangered children, but that might not be enough to stop them from breaking the rules by falling in love. (978-1-63555-292-8)

**Unexpected Partners** by Michelle Larkin. Dr. Chloe Maddox tries desperately to deny her attraction for Detective Dana Blake as they flee from a serial killer who's hunting them both. (978-1-63555-203-4)